Joan O'D
Midlands
always writing freelance while in other
occupations. Her previous published
works include three novels and three
collections of short stories. She is now
retired and lives in Oxford.

Author photograph by Pauline Lord

Argument with an East Wind

Joan O'Donovan

BLACK SWAN

ARGUMENT WITH AN EAST WIND

A BLACK SWAN BOOK   0 552 99282 8

Originally published in Great Britain by
Macmillan London Limited

PRINTING HISTORY

Macmillan London edition published 1986
Black Swan edition published 1988

This book is set in 11/12 pt Century
by Colset Private Limited, Singapore.

Black Swan Books are published by
Transworld Publishers Ltd., 61–63
Uxbridge Road, Ealing, London W5 5SA, in
Australia by Transworld Publishers
(Australia) Pty. Ltd., 15–23 Helles Avenue,
Moorebank, NSW 2170, and in
New Zealand by Transworld Publishers
(N.Z.) Ltd., Cnr. Moselle and Waipareira
Avenues, Henderson, Auckland.

Printed and bound by
The Guernsey Press Co. Ltd., Guernsey, Channel Islands.

FOR JOHN

There is no good arguing with the inevitable. The only argument available with an east wind is to put on your overcoat.

JAMES RUSSELL LOWELL

Argument with an East
Wind

1

Eva stirred, woke briefly, puzzled about her bed – which bed? – and the framed square of less-dense dark, then closed her eyes again.

It was not true that the war was over. There were enemy troops in Alsace, which was also part of north-west London, and the government had posted bills warning of a red alert. She could not see clearly because someone had tampered with the light yet was afraid to mend the connection in case she got a shock. The Chief gave her a key so that she could work in head office after all; but she found that the decorators had white-washed the archives and that the retrieval mechanism was out of true. There was a red poster on her desk, but it was also a playbill featuring Noël Coward and a foreign actress whose name she couldn't decipher. The title of the piece stood out vividly: *Hélas, la Reine!* Then she found herself on a desert island and knew that she was a prisoner of war and that she was to clear up the litter from the driftline; but when she touched it she encountered soil from a stopped-up drain, and as she shrank away in disgust a time-bomb exploded under her hand.

Eva jerked violently and her eyes shot open. The car backfired again and she turned her head, listening as it drove away. A window. Her own. And it was bright with morning. So she wasn't marooned. After all her wanderings she was back in her own bed, safe.

Safe? Still uneasy, her heart pounding, she tried to pin down those vivid dissolving shapes. Something about the royal family, was it? Or a blind woman lost in a Hampstead cul-de-sac?

But it was too late. Dispersing like steam, the nightmare edged and curled away seeking to evade her scrutiny, leaving no more than the burden of its distress inert on her diaphragm as Pussy, her old cat, had liked to lie. The insubstantial pageant, faded, had left not a rack behind – or nothing you could reasonably call a rack, she told Pussy in passing.

Eva could smell that it had rained; but now the sun was up and rinsing her room with watercolour light, May-time light, transparent, opalescent almost, nothing like the unambiguous golden syrup she had known for the past three weeks. A scent of lilac came to her; and the sawing note of a wren, more voice than feathers, who was throwing about what weight he had in her front garden.

So she was home. Stale, grubby, jet-worn, perhaps even a mite deflated, but undeniably home. Yes, and with no need now to go rushing out because it was Monday and there was her desk to clear before a new week came flooding in. Your time's your own, she reminded herself, and don't you forget it, my girl: for twenty-four hours a day, seven days a week, you can do what you bloody well choose.

'So yo, ho, ho!' she added aloud as a flicker of panic stirred in her.

She lay for a while and thought about it. Job? Non-job? Had it been a non-job, hers? She supposed it had, in a manner of speaking. It all depended, of course, on which manner of speaking. Nora's, for instance: *Ten years down the drain, ye great soft eejut, and now look where it's got you!*

Ten years down the drain. And now look where it had got her. Well, it was a point of view.

Impatiently, Eva hitched up on to one elbow and leant out to see the time; then, 'Oh, my sainted cat!' she whimpered as the hangover snarled back at her from its kennel in her skull. The clock said five to four.

She lowered herself gently as though on to egg-shells. Five to four? Five to *four*? Madness. She shut her eyes.

A plane ripped low over the roof and, wincing against its slate-pencil screech, she remembered then that she'd stopped the clock three weeks before; how, with the taxi waiting to take her to the airport, she'd rushed upstairs in a last-minute flurry and disconnected it. To save electricity. An economy. Because she was now sixty and what she refused to call a senior citizen and why the hell should she?

But sixty! She, Eva Wootton, an OAP! Good grief, that'd take some getting used to!

She giggled briefly at the thought, began to hum 'Maybe it's because I'm a pinchoner', broke off. The gang had enjoyed her song all right, but it no longer struck her as funny. Not that there was anything wrong with the lines. The lines were fine; it was the reality which stuck in her gullet – that same reality which had smitten her when, with no more than the tweak of a plug from a socket, she had arrested time, as if for ever, at five minutes to four in the afternoon and, in spite of the taxi ticking away pound notes at her gate, had paused to mourn the fluid passing of her days and the gutters down which they ran.

Eva sighed. So there you are, she told Pussy. All that splendid *Weltschmerz*, the impressive new leaves we were going to turn. And what do we do about it? We get drunk.

Reflected light shimmered on the ceiling like water over ribbed and sunlit sand, and at once joy spurted, making her smile. Then the smile changed to a grin. Economy? When it hadn't even occurred to her to cancel the taxi and hop on a bus?

A ring-dove was moaning in a garden over the way. Dis-*gus*-ting, dis-*gus*-ting. And so I am, Eva agreed cheerfully. Haven't I everything to live for? Aren't I, in a manner of speaking, lucky?

She shut her eyes again the better to think about Alec.

* * *

Eva lurched awake, the burden back with her. Three weeks ago, distanced from it by a world which tilted giddily at the tip of a wing, she'd shuffled anxiety off; but now she was home, the dalliance over. This was reality. There was to be no more dodging of facts. She was a statutory old person and she'd slung in her job five years before she need have done. So how about that for starters? she asked Pussy.

Her hand went out, felt for the clock, tapped it reassuringly as she might the arm of a friend; for it, too, was frozen in the past, a past that had indeed gone. When she set it going again it would be to measure the future, hers. A future she'd let herself be manoeuvred into. The scrap-heap.

Wryly, she thought of the Chief's farewell letter: devoted service, integrity, unfailing loyalty, an inspiration to all who knew you. . . . But, William S. apart, who was more aware than she that gobbets like this were fashioned to slither without cerebration or feeling from any dictating tongue? Yet had she torn it up, that insult of a letter, with the contempt it deserved? No, she had not. She'd returned again and again, sieving it for just one sentence, one, which she could recognise as real; something – anything – to help her believe that she hadn't, after all, wasted those years, that she – Eva, unique – had not gone unregarded.

She hadn't found it. Mr Salwart's well-honed praise did nothing but diminish her further; and as for his explanation of why, whether she went or stayed, her post was to be axed. . . . Oh, resounding words they were, all of them, words implying grave debate and a weight of judgement; but what did it actually mean, *the inevitable reassessment of our priorities taking cognisance of technological expansion during a period of planned non-growth?* It meant that Eva Wootton was out and a word processor in.

So, all right, they'd have gone on paying her for another five years, yes, and found little tasks for her to fill her time with – like hell they would, given the chance! But she didn't give them the chance. Instead, she slammed in her resignation to bring them to their senses. Because they all knew – even Lionel Salwart knew – that she, Eva, was good at things which a machine couldn't even begin to tackle. Like slipping in, unprogrammed, the right word to the right person at the right moment. Like exposing the thorn of truth which a bouquet of compliments had been arranged to conceal. Like showing impulsive pity, being generous. Like – yes, Alec Burroughs, late of the parish of All Souls, Hammel-on-Sea – like being capable of love.

So there it was. It might have been a non-job, hers, as Nora said; but, by God, she'd made something of it. Like a real job, for instance. And of course the scales would fall from their eyes when they saw that she meant it; and of course they'd come running, horrified, to call her back.

'Only they didn't call me back,' she told the ceiling. 'They let me go.'

Her retirement would be a saving, and they'd jumped at a chance to save. So much for Eva.

A sigh built up in her, a sigh as big as a house. They'd known her for what she was, a great soft eejut, too hurt to make a fuss, too proud to stand on her rights, too quirky to join a union. She could almost smell their relief when she gave up, and their scorn because she'd made it so easy for them. And she minded, that was the humiliating thing; she really minded. Still, ten years of Eva Wootton had been invested in that non-job. Ten years! How could she not mind?

Ten years. And, before Tigby, Garchester. It was a long time since she'd let herself remember Garchester or think of life before Alec.

Alec. . . .

Off went the duvet in one resolute sweep, and erect, purposeful, she sat on the edge of the bed cautiously stretching her neck while her feet paddled in the rug to find their slippers; then she gave her belly a friendly slap – all that lovely food, she mourned, all that

15

drink! – then went to the dressing table and picked up her watch. Twenty to seven. That was more like it. Twenty to seven on a fine May morning when it could, after all, have been raining frogs – why not? – not to mention what happened to Sodom and Gomorrah. Because don't tell me, she challenged, that the Almighty's all that cheered by the goings-on in Tigby, either.

Alec's latest card, grubby and softened from much handling, lay where she had put it before going to bed. She touched it, looking tenderly at the dreadful picture – poor Alec, how she cringed for him! – a fluffy puppy waving bye-bye to a fluffy kitty, the caption *Bon Voyage*. On the back was typed: *Have just heard about your hols. Lucky old you. Have fun and don't do anything I wouldn't. A.*

Her smile broadened. Cautious bastard! Not even to write 'love' or sign his name! Still smiling, she tucked the card into the frame of the mirror and, sitting down, began to brush her hair.

Nora. That was the first thing she'd do, take Nora's present, go early. . . .

But Eva sat on, exploring her face for those signs of change which her eye was now so quick to detect. There was hardly any grey, certainly not enough to dull its fairness, but how fine her hair had grown, how insubstantial, and how pink that scalp which – oh, insidiously – was beginning to show through. Perhaps one day she'd be nearly bald like Nora, of whom she had suddenly been reminded. Her tan suited her, though; there was nothing wrong with that – nor should there be, by God! And at the recollection of how much it had cost, that tan, her blood chilled. Just how many unplugged clocks would it take to pay for that robust gesture of contempt, those two fingers thrust up in defiance of age and loss? But she'd do it again, yes, given the occasion. Because to go out smiling, chin high, with panache when they thought she was defeated – that made her feel it was something, after all, to be Eva Wootton.

A street door slammed – number seven. Ollie Tucker always walked to the station to catch the eight-o-five and he always slammed the door, which, back in the old days like last month, had been her signal to finish breakfast. A car came down the road. Another. A third. The paper-boy scooted his bike along the pavement and someone shouted to him to stop it. Barnes Farm Close was coming to life.

Standing by the window Eva marvelled at the day. Everything was yeasty with life, abundant, prodigal. In her absence the hedge had boiled up and over like thick green soup and the may tree become one vast raspberry inflorescence. As she watched, a blond and shaggy mongrel rounded the corner, purposeful, jaws laughing, tail as wide as an otter's. Eva called, but, intent on love or breakfast, Topaz padded past flourishing her feathers like a boa.

England, she told Pussy. We couldn't be anywhere else. And they fanned out in memory like a feverish scatter of snapshots, those so different places which, a mere ten hours before, she had left behind. Beaches cliffed by blinding white hotels. Dazzling ribbons of glare unspooling in dust. Limpet villages high on forgotten mountains; and, like some great rag-bag, the olive-groves, car parks, cafés, vineyards, cathedrals, supermarkets, palaces and factories tumbled together with pillars among which Helen might have walked, all compacted into a span which defied history and all, all blurred by wine and chatter and by the ubiquitous, the bruising sun. Non-travel, she told Pussy, joke-travel; like my non and joke you know what.

Eva walked restlessly round the room, sat down again before the mirror, her eyes on Alec's card. True, but there were worse anaesthetics than joke-travel. To have been a digit in that sum of corporate living, to have found communion in smoothing lotion over a raw-meat back and in turn accepted the cooling hand, that was something; and to have put down her burden for a while, to have grown confident that life might, after all,

17

go her way – under that amazing sun how could she believe other? – wasn't that something, too? For surely, surely, at the end of things there was some kind of sense, a pattern in which all those apparently disastrous choices of her life would take their royal place. If one willed the right – as she did, though imperfectly – how could any mistake be irretrievable, any misunderstanding irreversible, any silence yet made which could not be broken?

On top of which – so her thoughts had run – a lot can happen in three weeks.

Three weeks! Wars had been won, women wooed, countries overthrown in less time than that; and what a little thing a letter was by comparison. Three weeks? Of course there'd be letters waiting when she got home. There were certain to be letters. Well, a letter.

So she'd tossed them away, those costly days; let them go, one by one, as though they were nothing. And now she was home.

Eva dropped her eyes, embarrassed by the hurt she saw mirrored in them. Letters? An open note, signed *luv, Archie and Moo*, telling her to pop round if she needed milk, bread, etc. A bulging envelope – she hadn't opened it – from Doris. Her polling card for the local government elections which she had, in any case, missed. Five picture postcards from ex-colleagues on holiday who affected to wish that she had been with them. A catalogue of bargain offers for goods she didn't want. The phone bill, the gas bill, the electricity bill, and a form asking which post office her pension should go to. The rest was silence.

Right! she'd instructed herself. Clean your teeth, then, and get to bed like a good girl.

Correction. Like a bad girl, with yet another gin and a sleeping pill. It was pitiful.

She got up and moved about the room, stopping to fondle the lump of driftwood, a paper-weight now, but turning back from the book-lined shelves. Odd, though, that survival should so often depend on trivia – she

18

caressed the wood again – trivia like hoping for the best, like looking on the funny side of little agonies, like counting one's blessings even when they were thinnish on the ground.

So go on, she encouraged, count the bloody things.

Blessings? She thought about it. All right, she'd been spared a move to the Dalek-drome the County had built out in the sticks on the pretext that it would save millions of pounds of ratepayers' money, dishonest buggers. She'd called it Salwart's Folly, and the name had stuck. Yes, and there had been some magical moments on that holiday, for all she might make fun of it – one particular night, huge moon in ribcage of cloud, when she'd had a feeling not so much of flying as of being blown like smoke across the world; and the morning when she and Latchy had gone to Olympia early and seen it in silence. And of course, yes, back to it again, the gang, that total in which, with willing passivity, she'd submerged herself: that, too, had been a blessing in its way. The gang in Italy, Greece. The gang, though rather the worse for wear, saying goodbye at Luton airport last night – was it only last night? The gang cheerful, confident, secure, determined to get its money's worth. Yes, she was going to miss the protection of the gang – or was it Latchy she was going to miss? They'd fitted together calmly, he and she, had found it simple to be easy with each other; and she could, by the end, have liked him a lot more than this companionable little had it not been for Alec. But Alec was there, rooted in her; and, though he was far away, and silent of late, and in any case not rightly hers to cherish, the thought of him held her back. She was, she supposed – observing what others got up to so lightly – an old-fashioned kind of woman; but trusting, being trusted, that wasn't a thing to tamper with. Not for a bit of easy fun. Not even for a bit of easy fun with a man like Latchy.

All the same, Latchy. . . .

Oh, but no letter! Once again no letter! Had Alec

really no news for her yet? There'd been plenty of postcards since he left. He'd smothered her with postcards.
Postcards to keep in touch but saying nothing in particular, which is what postcards are for; but as for a real
letter, it was nearly nine months since he'd sent
one – not that she could blame him for that: he was
trying to be fair, as best he could, in an impossible
situation. But nine months! She could have borne him a
child. Had she not been sixty, of course. An old woman.
A bloody OAP.

She mopped angrily at her eyes. A child? What was
she thinking of! Alec had children enough without any
more from her.

2

Eva was in the bath when she heard the milk-float and remembered, damn, that she'd left no note for Bob. She started for the stairs, dragging on a flimsy wrap which clung to her wet skin. Just in time. Bob, his back to her, stooped to the Johnsons' porch, which was adjacent to her own with no more than knee-high privet between; and, 'Boo!' Eva said, leaning over to speak in his ear. Then, 'Oh dear,' she added. 'Sorry!' Grinned deprecatingly, felt foolish.

For once, Bob wasn't alone. A young man came lounging after him, lean, a face like sulky rubber. She tried to include the stranger in the joke but, unsmiling, he stared her out.

She'd startled Bob, though, the old stick. He jerked violently then, with care, deposited two of the three bottles in his splayed hands before turning round.

'Y'oughtn't to have done that, Mrs Wootton,' he said aggrieved. 'I nearly dropped the milk.'

He'd seen Alec leaving the house one morning long ago and had called her 'missis' ever since. Sometimes he asked if her hubby was still abroad.

'Y'oughtn't to have done that,' he repeated.

'Sorry, Bob, I. . . .'

But Bob's face had changed. Lids fluttering, eyes skidding away in a kind of old-maidish swoon, he was pretending not to see what he saw. Human parts.

Blushing herself then, but out of vexation, Eva tugged at her gaping robe. She recalled with sudden nostalgia those shining beaches where Gwen alone of

21

all the gang went into contortions lest anyone should glimpse her skinny bum. But now she was back at the centre of the moral universe, Tigby, where ladies called breasts 'the bust' and never said 'bum'. She must try to remember.

Holding close the edges of her wrap from her throat to a place she could think only of a rude name for, Eva said placatingly: 'I forgot to leave a note. . . .'

Bob leant over – not too close – and put the spare bottle on her step.

'I carried one up for you every time. Y'know, in case you was back. I always 'ad a look.' He smiled at her, shy. 'And the milk was 'andy if you was.'

The young man yawned, shifted his weight to the other hip.

'Thanks, Bob; that was kind of you.' She glanced uncertainly at the stranger. 'Everything OK?'

'Yeah, yeah. And you still want your usual, Mrs Wootton?'

'Please.'

Bob's manner became self-important.

'I got an assistant now. I'm learning him. Make a note, 'Arry: number one Barnes Farm Close, a pint Monday, Wednesday, Friday and Sat'dy. I 'aven't forgot, have I, Mrs Wootton?' he said, pleased. ''Ere,' he added to Harry, 'I thought I told you to write that down.'

'I shan't forget, Dad.'

'Are you Bob's son?' she asked the boy, surprised.

'My son? Not likely!' Bob was flustered. 'I 'aven't got no son no more'n he hasn't got no manners. But he don't forget things, I'll give 'im that. Live and let live's my motto.'

'Hello, Harry,' Eva said, friendly, over her clamped right hand.

'Don't expect no chit-chat from 'im; 'e ain't got no feelings. Still,'e could've gone to college – yeah, I'll give 'im that – only 'e didn't see no point.' He looked indignantly at the youth. ''Ere, where's your manners?

Mrs Wootton's an old customer – how long now, Mrs Wootton?'

'Ten years last Christmas, Bob.'

'Ten? Cor! And ain't you brown, eh? I bet your 'ubby was glad to see you.'

'Sunshine all the way!' Eva carolled ignoring the reference to Alec. 'And with time to enjoy it now I've retired,' she told him smiling.

Retired! The word still came as a shock.

'Nice you can be so 'appy about it.'

'But of course!' she lied, beating back a sudden access of despair.

'Not like my old man, then.'

'What about him?'

'When the company told 'im 'e was past it 'e done 'isself in.'

'What?' Eva said, startled.

'Yeah,' Bob said, kindling under her interest. 'First 'e took his 'olidays – well, that was only right: 'e'd earned 'is 'olidays, so 'e took 'em. Went to Skegness, I think it was – or was it Margate? No, Skegness – then 'e come back, see; and the first day 'ome, like it might be you today, Mrs Wootton, 'e blew out 'is brains with that little old gun as 'e used for potting at rabbits. Marvellous, innit? Didn't even tell Mum. Nah, 'e just 'ad a good breakfast – 'e always did 'ave a good breakfast, Dad did; a proper cooked one, I'll give 'im that. . . .'

'Aw, Christ!' Harry muttered.

'And?' Eva encouraged, glaring at the young man.

'Then 'e shot 'isself – I told you. Still, live and let live, that's my motto. It takes all sorts. But you're the cheerful type, I reckon, eh? I bet you got an 'obby. It keeps you young, an 'obby. Like me wiv my trains.'

'*Trains*, Bob?'

'Yeah. Y'know, models. Y'oughter come and see my trains. Be nice,' he told her kindly, 'when your 'ubby's 'ome for good.'

'Won't it,' Eva said brightly. 'Well, I mustn't keep you. . . .'

'This where the niggers live?' she heard Harry ask as they turned away.

'Yeah. Number three Barnes Farm Close, two pints Monday to Friday, four pints and a dozen eggs and a small double cream Sat'dy. Never varies.'

'She show them her titties, too?' he called to Bob, who was hurrying ahead.

Eva shrugged as she picked up the bottle from the step. Bienvenu à Tigby, Pussy, site paléolithique.

She glanced back as the float started up and saw that Harry had lingered in the Johnsons' garden.

'What the hell . . .?'

He straightened up with two fistfuls of tulips torn from the soil.

'Niggers,' he said, and spat, tossing the bulbs on to the lawn.

Rage flooded her. Wrap flying, milk-bottle lifted like a torch, Eva plunged down the garden path.

'You come back here . . .!'

But her robe tangled with an overgrown briar which all but tweaked it off her back. She clutched at it, dropped the bottle, lost her balance and fell heavily into the bushes. By the time she'd struggled to her feet Harry had gone, leaving the Johnsons' gate wide open.

'Damn, damn, *damn* . . .!'

A curtain twitched in the house across the way – that would be Mrs Locked-bolted-and-barred; he was at work. Eva glared back at the unseen eyes which were watching her. Once inside, she slammed her front door and leant against it, sick with disgust. Poor Miriam, poor Ed. And they took such a pride in their garden. She'd go round, try to explain. . . . Not easy, though; not easy.

It struck her then that it was a long time since she'd seen the Johnsons to talk to – about a year, she supposed: she hadn't had the heart to initiate much since Alec left. But now, yes, of course she must. . . .

She examined the soiled wrap, her grazed leg, scratched arms. What a way to celebrate her first day home!

The word pulled her up. Home? Wasn't that supposed to be where the heart was? She pondered it as she trailed back to the bathroom.

3

So what was she going to do with today? It was hers and empty; and they could so easily slip through her fingers, those minutes, those hours, leaving nothing but a deposit of waste and regret. At least she'd learnt that. Which, she consoled herself, went on the credit side of the old-age balance-sheet. One knew one's weaknesses by now; one had them taped. It might be wry comfort, but it was comfort of a sort.

'No more nasty shocks,' she told Pussy.

It was like promising herself a treat.

And why not? Jove's thunderbolts were bad enough – like the axing of her post, like Alec's continued remoteness – but in the end time and reason would deal with these. Alec would write when he was free to say what they both wanted to hear – of that she was certain – and this interim silence was no more than a stressful part of the same pact. As for her job – meaning the panic emptiness of a week without its accustomed structures, meaning her wounded pride – all she had to do was accept that they could get along without her, refuse to be idle, then – wow! And there she was, she saw herself, dancing through those days fountaining white joy because they were now her own.

No, it wasn't the blows from without which were the killers; real danger lay within – for oh, the black holes into which one might fall, those treacherous inadequacies! Because, when it came to it, who could inflict damage half so frightening as the destructive violation one wreaked on oneself? And to be old, to have charted the hazards, that made for peace – well, a dented peace – and, yes, she must be grateful.

Which was all very fine. Noble sentiments, luscious words – but what about today, Monday, which, somehow, had to be got through? And why choose this of all moments to remember that that incompetent tart Lorraine Hampstead had rocketed up the promotion ladder in that new job of hers? Or so Angela had said. But there, L.H. was only half her age and oh, she remarked to Pussy, the difference to me.

'So let's pull ourselves together, my esteemed cat,' Eva said aloud, 'fill each unforgiving minute with sixty seconds' worth of distance run. Mr Kipling does make exceedingly good. . . . Which reminds me – shopping list.'

Doris's letter was on the kitchen counter where she'd tossed it early that morning, and her hand went out. But, no, she wouldn't open it, not now – she took up the pad and biro instead – she wouldn't open it or any other till she'd opened Alec's, so there. Then, childish! she scolded. As if not reading other people's letters would hurry his along! All the same, her heart lifted a little as though she had stumbled on a kind of magic to bring Alec near.

'You're a very silly woman,' she said, beginning to write.

```
*Nora        *post OAP
             form              *bread
             *cash t.          *butter/eggs/
             cheques           cheese
                               *gn veg/pots/
                               fruit
                               *chops
```

Chops? She crossed off the *s*. Better not get ideas above her station. Milk, though – damn Harry. And that seemed to be it. So how about a quick coffee, then dress and go out? But why was the house so quiet? She'd never before noticed how very silent. . . .

At once Eva wrinkled her nose. *Very* silent? Sorry, Idris, 'silent' will, of course, do.

She lit the gas under the kettle – enough water for one mug only. Thy name is economy – and as she turned away glimpsed the garden through the side window.

But how mindless to be sweating over a stupid list when she hadn't been out to look at her garden! She ran through to the dining room where an inert mass of air met her smelling of some forgotten soup; which, as she wrestled with the bolt of the french door, made her exclaim that she was right, Pussy, it was as she'd always suspected: their wicked Auntie Breem did not air the house properly when Mother was away.

Pussy. It was ridiculous the way she still talked to that damned cat. For Pussy had died nearly a year ago, had died just after Alec left. What remained of Pussy was buried under the plum tree which stood in the middle of the waving grass she chose to call a lawn.

'And you needn't start getting sentimental about him, either,' she said aloud. 'Your late cat was subnormal and you know it, the smelly old thing. You only tolerated his foul ways because Alec gave him to you that Christmas. Didn't even bother to give him a name, did you . . .?'

Well, no name. She and Pussy had at least had that in common.

So now the wych-elm was dead, too. She stood before it, defeated. Someone had told her – who was it? – that sometimes a sucker would grow belatedly and the tree re-establish itself – but, no, that was the common elm, surely? How ignorant she was about these important things. Could it happen with a wych-elm? So far there was no greening hope. It was like those dear, dead days beyond recall which the people who'd brought her up used to embarrass her by singing about as they leant together over the piano on a Sunday evening while she accompanied them and blushed when they held hands.

She'd thought the Woottons too old for love, poor things; and now she could have given them ten, fifteen years.

The wych-elm might be dead but the Christmas tree was fine. It still flourished where Alec had planted it over ten years before; and Eva smiled to see the year's new growth, light on dark. Ten years. Would the next ten go so fast? She'd be seventy then. Seventy? Impossible! She couldn't begin to imagine herself being seventy, couldn't envisage herself being really old at all. She was a bit low at the moment, true, not quite on form; but on good days how it sparkled still, how it leapt and sprang, that fountain of perennial youth which was Eva Wootton.

Still smiling, she stroked the striated green, the tender and the dark, remembering that first Christmas in Tigby. She'd moved the day before Christmas Eve, full of foreboding, turbulent with doubt. Why had she bought the house anyway, raw and unlovely on the corner of a desolate building site? And, if she must buy the house and its accompanying mud, why take on that extra land as well merely to oblige those end-on strangers in the next road who wanted no more than what they called a patio? She must have been mad. She was mad. Oh, and the bleakness of it all, the naked light-bulbs, the smell of size and her furniture huddling moodily, eyeing the spaces between. What a welcome for Alec – two mugs, two plates, a bottle of champagne and some turkey sandwiches from British Rail! Woe, woe, it was all a dreadful mistake. Even the holly on the front door looked funereal. And would Alec, in any case, come? He said he'd try – which, poor darling, was all he could say – so how could one guess? Certainly she dared not bank on it; but, hungry as she was, wretched as she was, late as it grew, she went on hoping.

Then, suddenly, he was there, paying off the taxi, kissing her. Alec with his hat on the back of his head, clutching the kitten which was Pussy. Alec, self-conscious with a Christmas tree – this Christmas tree – which he must have stopped to decorate in a fever of love and clumsiness before catching the last train from Garchester. She'd never valued a present more than that runt of a tree with its garish tinsel and hideous, squinting, top-heavy fairy doll. And nothing would do him, no, but that they should plant it there and then, for where among screwed-up newspaper and packing cases was there a place festive enough? But with Orion up and a full moon rising it would shine in the rubble like a queen.

So Alec had borrowed a spade from the Johnsons and they'd gone out together with mugs of champagne and planted it just as it was, tinsel, baubles, fairy doll and all. She could have cried for that doll, it was so ugly, so dear, so Alec. She could have cried for happiness because he had come and misery because he would have to go – well, of course he'd have to go: his wife was still in Garchester and Alec hadn't broken with Jean yet.

But Alec hated tears so she didn't cry. She'd gone on grinning at him – merry, merry – trying not to think about his going, trying to keep her sense of impending loss from leaking through, telling herself that it couldn't be long now before things were sorted out.

So 'Happy Christmas, darling!' she'd cried, raising the mug marked *Hers*, gesturing for him to raise the mug marked *His*.

Alec had looked back at her, not smiling but with an expression on his face which, glimpsed by moonlight, made Eva still. In that moment everything – yes, even her sacrifice – became radiantly worth while. He said, almost laconic: 'I'm saving my greetings till the right day.'

She dared not speak. He slid an arm round her.

'Christmas morning – early Christmas morning, darling. I think Santa must have got my letter after all because he's given me Eva Wootton for Christmas.'

And, unbelievably, Alec had stayed not just for the hour or two of their need but for five days and six nights, the longest stretch of time they had ever spent

30

together. He had busied himself about the house and, pipe in mouth, put up the curtains, hung her pictures, mended the defective catch on the side door; and she remembered now in her body, vividly, the waking, the touching, the being aware even in sleep of those slackly-encompassing limbs which quickened as she stirred.

How few such nights there had been.

She sighed, and at once smiled as she recalled Alec's hangdog look when daylight revealed their foolishness – the tinsel so tawdry, the doll awry, the clay caked on their shoes. Old idiots, he'd said, both of them. Yes, but she that sad bit older an idiot than he. Not, good God, that it mattered, no, except perhaps to the way she felt now.

Ten years ago last Christmas. Those end-on strangers with the patio had long since been Archie and Moo and the scarred earth her garden; but as for things being sorted out. . . .

Eva sighed again, looked about her. Weeds – how they'd thrust up in her absence! Still, they were vigorous and each one in its unique way beautiful. . . . Oh, leave them, let them be, she counselled Pussy. The ghost of Pussy. The bones of Pussy under the plum tree which stood, a green and ossified fountain, in the middle of the garden.

Ten years. How had it happened? How had they let it happen? Had they, when it came to it, had any choice? Had anyone any choice, ever?

But thank heaven she'd bought that extra bit of land. It was the best part of the garden; and in that sheltered alcove Eva stopped and tilted her face to the sun.

'Nice!' she exclaimed, approving the scratched enamel of the sky, the golden disc, the pulse of radiance in the rosebuds; and suddenly, against reason, she found herself transformed into a vessel for joy. Back went her head and, arms all-blessing, she burst into a vibrant imitation of Ella Fitzgerald.

'When ah get to heaven gonna put on mah weeds,

Gonna stomp all over God's heaven!
Hea-vern! Hea-*vern* . . .!'

Then hand over mouth, clamp! Eva cast a horrified glance at the Johnsons' house. Oh my God, Pussy, we've done it again!

But no; even if she were home, Miriam couldn't possibly have heard. There wasn't a single window open; which was odd, but a relief, for if they'd taken her bit of nonsense personally. . . . As they well might, Eva supposed, Tigby being what it was. Which would be awful, Miriam and Ed being the best neighbours one could wish for – as she'd been at some pains to tell Jack Thornby that time he'd come creeping round after dark campaigning to keep Tigby white.

Contemptible bastard! It still made her grin to rehearse the two-year-old memory of that encounter.

'Miss Wootton?' His manner was confident.

'Yes?' she'd said, wondering why this man, whoever he was, had a scarf round his face and how he knew her name.

'I'm speaking in my private capacity on behalf of a number of fellow Tigbeians – all highly influential men, I might say, Miss Wootton – who believe the time has come, nay, more than come, to put a stop to this insidious invasion of our shores by foreigners. . . .'

She was genuinely puzzled. 'Foreigners?'

'Aye.' A lowering of the voice. 'Pakis and niggers, not to put too fine a point on it. You've some next door, or so I hear; and this is a nice residential area. Have you thought what's going to happen when you want to sell your house, eh? That's why I'm here. If you'd like to add your signature to this petition. . . .'

Is this anger? she'd wondered, trying not to tremble, struggling to deal with her murderous disgust. So: 'Come in,' she'd said. 'No, but I insist. You did, after all, ring my bell.'

And brushing aside his reluctance, refusing to accept his excuses, Eva had taken his arm and as good as forced him through to where they were sitting, Miriam and Ed, looking as wholesome and shiny as two cherished black boots. And Alec was sitting there, too, of course; Alec who'd happened to drop in on the spur of the moment hoping to find her alone.

'Mr and Mrs Johnson,' she'd told him, 'good friends of mine – and how lucky I am to have such marvellous neighbours.'

Then, in an impersonal voice, she'd stated Thornby's business. Stated it loud and clear.

For that's who it was, Jack Thornby – *Councillor* Jack Thornby; and therein lay the rub, for it turned out that he and Alec knew each other well. In the way of business.

In focus, sharp-edged, that scene was as vivid still as her recollection of the squinting fairy doll: the Johnsons trying to smile, uncertain how to behave; Alec doing his best to imply that although he happened to be in Miss Wootton's house they'd never met socially; Thornby blinking under the light, his clipboard behind his back, impersonating a man who might possibly have come to read the meter. . . .

'My finest hour, Pussy,' she said as she stretched up to tweak a dead spray from the laburnum.

Yes, but after that finest hour had come Alec's rage – not only their first serious quarrel but also a depth charge, appalling, incomprehensible. Would she do such a thing again, knowing he'd react like this? She hoped she would, thought she might – but, no, she still didn't understand.

And the Johnsons? Suddenly, it occurred to Eva to wonder what they'd felt. They'd never thanked her for championing them, and neither had referred to the incident again. But they must have spoken of it to each other. So what had they said? Uneasy, she wished she'd thought to ask herself that question before.

And now Jack Thornby – Councillor Jack Thornby – like Pussy, like the wych-elm, was dead and Alec had gone North. Of the people who really mattered to her only Nora and the Johnsons remained.

Eva added another seed-pod to the pile on her palm and sighed as she shook her head at him, that man of hers, that man of Jean's. Screaming that she was only his secretary; that Thornby was an elected member, useful. Useful! As if that entitled him to a larger share of human rights than Miriam and Ed. As if to be a secretary meant she wasn't to speak her mind.

It was a week, more, before Alec was easy with her again; then he turned up one evening as though nothing had happened – indeed, seemed wounded that she should recall the incident. When had he lost his temper? Oh, that day! But, darling, he'd had a dreadful time with those idiot architects; and then to come round and find she wasn't alone. . . . *Only his secretary?* He'd said no such thing! Did she *seriously* imagine . . .? Nor had he said Thornby could be useful to him – well, not meaning what she was implying, though he might well in the heat of the moment. . . .

She'd long since forgotten what he might well have said in the heat of the moment; but she hadn't forgotten that he'd said 'only his secretary', nor 'useful'.

'Poor Alec!' she whispered, sad for him, humiliated with him because she'd seen his weakness exposed. Well, there it was. Time's sediment.

She tossed the dead blossoms on to the compost-heap and moved towards the house. Good God, she wasn't even dressed yet!

'Coo-ee! Ee-va!'

Eva walked on, hoping Moo might think she hadn't heard. She was in no mood for Moo, who settled on the spirits like a porridge poultice. All the same. . . . And, guiltily, she remembered the welcome home card which had gone straight into the bin.

At the same moment she remembered something else, the kettle. When she opened her door it was on to a reek of charred enamel. So much for economy.

4

So 'OUT!' she told herself, impatient now, niggling to
be on the go, to get back into the mainstream of life.
Meaning Tigby High Street? Meaning Tigby High
Street. At least it was out.

Astonishingly, she wasn't tired. Extraordinary,
that. Too much to eat, too much to drink, too short a
night and too much on her mind, yet she didn't feel
tired. Not in the least. Well, not very. Not what you
could actually call *tired*.

Oh, but such a mess! A suitcase disgorging clothes
like suds over the carpet; her travel-bag arrested in a
gargantuan yawn. Which reminded her – t. cheques.

It was while looking for them that she came on the
photograph of the gang at the gang's special table. But
the gang's special table where? She sat down to ponder
the question. And was it Antonio, Mario, Stavros or
Michel who beamed so possessively down, napkin
folded, bottle aloft? Ah, that moustache; it was Mario.
Where, though, was another matter. There had been so
many places.

'How wonderful we look,' Eva marvelled, 'how
happy!'

It was true. Everyone was sunburnt, most were
handsome and not all that old, really, when you came
to think of it; except for Gwen, who appeared to be a
hundred and sinking fast. Serve her right, Puss! Wash
your hands, blow your nose, join the queue, that's not
quite nice. . . . So many things in Gwen's book weren't
quite nice.

And in the middle of the picture, Latchy. Latchy with one arm cuddling her, the other trying without success to get round Gwen.

On the back of the photo were phone numbers, addresses, invitations to take pot luck, exhortations to meet again – next year, before Christmas, for a day in Town, as soon as possible. Because they must keep in touch. As of course they would. Of course.

Still squinting at the print, Eva shrugged her way into an old cotton dress. Then, impulsively, she plumped herself down on the edge of the bed and dialled Latchy's number, repeating them under her breath, those as yet strange digits, memorising the sum.

Latchy. The outline of his face was clear in her mind – those sardonic lion-coloured eyes, the crooked mouth, the scarred and bunchy chin; and when the phone began to ring in that faraway house which she didn't yet know Eva smiled, her lips already parted to reply. She might have promised not to ring Alec but there was no reason why she shouldn't ring Latchy. It would be good to speak to someone – already she regretted her flight from Moo.

The bell drilled on and on. After a while it seemed to turn into a gigantic instrument of demolition. Half-hypnotised, she imagined plaster flying in flakes from the walls. Surely the house would topple, the eye be full of grit as the roof caved in, the whole street collapse in shattered brick and a smoke of rising dust.

The chimes from All Saints cut across her fantasy and, counting them, she hung up. Eleven? It couldn't be eleven! But it was, the morning nearly over.

She thrust the photograph into the drawer of her bedside table. Handbag? The old white one would do. Still struggling with her zip she ran downstairs, the bag between her teeth. Had she got everything? T. cheques, wallet, OAP form, carrier-bag, keys. . . .

She glanced again at the wych-elm whose branches bared their uselessness to the sky like those terrible beggars in .... Where? Athens? Rome? Corinth?

36

Rhodes? Shaming, Pussy, not even to remember which.

No two ways about it, though: that tree would have to come down.

Oh, but the sun, the smells of summer! Childhood smells. The promise of a lifetime of fine mornings.

Smiling, head high, Eva savoured it all.

5

Marty Pike was delighted to see her. He wiped his eyes
over her from the back of the shop, then came purring
forward to serve her out of turn.

He ought to be ashamed of himself, she thought,
scandalised. Yes, and so ought she – preening herself
in his pleasure, not displeased to be singled out even by
Marty Pike and after all that had happened.

'So you found the sunshine, my dear?' he was saying.

'Yes,' she said cautiously, sniffing around for a double
meaning, 'there was plenty of sun.'

For one didn't trust Marty Pike – God, no! Everything he did was ambivalent, like creeping up on a
woman while he was reciting the Ten Commandments
and trying to get her to take her knickers off. And
always with some glib excuse like the exception prov-
ing the rule.

He threw out a damaged banana. Ostentatiously, he
selected the best.

'Your tan suits you.' He ran his eye over what he
could see of it. 'You're looking very nice, my dear.'

Eva smiled, non-committal. What had misled her in
the past was that he didn't look like a Don Giovanni;
and what with his asthma and bronchitis she'd never
credited him with the stamina. Besides, people could be
very spiteful, and there were those in Tigby who
remembered – or said they did – that Marty's father
had made a packet on the black market during the last
war and still nourished a grudge against his son
because they hadn't had what they considered to be

their rightful share of oranges. So, no, she might have disliked him but she'd never have believed a word of what was whispered about Marty and women; it would all have flowed over her and that would have been the end of it, had Marty not made one great mistake. He'd had a go at her.

A deft spin closed the paper bag. Anything else – tenderly – my dear? Gn veg, please.

She'd been properly caught off her guard that time; yes, and – she might as well admit it – scared. But she'd managed to keep her head. Kicked out hard and gone on smiling even as she bit him, as though this were no more than some rather brutal parlour game which she was keen to win. She'd even chatted him up. Or tried to.

But for all his skimpy chest Marty was surprisingly strong in the arm; and how bruising she found them, those heavy male bones which, since she wouldn't accept their favours, seemed determined to vanquish and insult: and just as she was thinking in rage and pain and disbelief, not rape, no, that's not possible, while knowing perfectly well it was, she managed to wrench herself clear. She took a proper uncluttered look at him then, the rutting old humbug with his high-minded words about the life force and his pitiful little chemistry set, and burst out laughing.

The spring cabbage, he was saying, had only just come in. It was still out the back – out *at* the back – but he'd be delighted to fetch some. Trouble? How could it be a trouble? It was a labour of love.

A Don Juan in long underwear smelling of liniment!

All the same, she hadn't meant to be quite so unkind, not go on and on laughing once the danger was past – for it was amazing how effective her sponta-neous laughter had been. But what a relief to laugh after being so scared; and how hard to stop – that is, until she saw he was really upset, upset enough to cry. She'd felt a brute then and, in a muddled way, both guilty and ashamed; because it's a painful thing to see a man cry, just as it goes against the grain of being a woman deliberately to leave a man disappointed. Even when you know you have to. Even when he's no right to expect anything else. Even when he's a shabby hypocrite who's damned well done his best to rape.

So what had she done? Rung the police? Denounced him to the vicar? Called in a witness while he was still in a tangle of braces and tears? She should, she supposed, have made some formal protest. But she hadn't, no; she'd given him a tissue and put on the kettle to make a cup of tea. She'd even painted arnica on the goose egg she'd raised on his shin and agonised over his bitten thumb, fool that she was. Why? Because he was so vulnerable, like some awful, unlovable child? Because he'd had a sad life? Because she disliked him so intensely? Because she was, after all, safe? Because he'd had the bloody nerve to ask her not to tell?

Eva squinted curiously at Marty Pike as he weighed out the greens. It had happened no more than two years before, just after the Thornby episode; but did Marty even remember? He gave no sign that he did. But, there, the human animal had a great capacity for refusing to face what it didn't want to know. All the relevant information was on file, of course, but sometimes those files had been buried almost beyond retrieval.

Well, she'd kept her word, had told nobody about the incident, not even Alec – least of all Alec.

'Sorry?' she asked, startled to find him mumbling by her ear.

'I said, pretty free and easy on the beaches, was it?' he repeated, handing her the change.

'Not particularly.' Eva's eye was cold.

'Ah. But you enjoyed your sun-bath this morning, I hear.'

'Sun-bath?'

'I understand', Marty remarked, sly, 'that a certain lady was seen topless in her own front garden.'

'Oh God!' Eva said, disgusted. 'The smaller the minds, Mr Pike –'

'Marty.'

'– Mr Pike, the bigger the mouths.'

His smile glinted at her. Gold in his teeth these days, had he?

'And haven't you anything else to say to me?'

'I don't think so, except goodbye. Oh, and thank you for the cheap grapes.'

'Goodbye, my dear,' he said, bland. 'Look after yourself.'

Not in the least put out. Assured, even. New suit, recent haircut, an air of having gone up in the world. Eva walked away, thoughtful. What else should she have had to say to him, for heaven's sake?

6

It was twelve-forty before Eva turned into Infirmary
Row where the Keepsake Home for the Aged was; but
since Nora always took lunch in her room the awkwardness of the hour didn't matter. Her visit wouldn't be
frowned on as, alas, so many things were. All the same,
she could have kicked herself. She'd wasted half the
morning doing nothing and then come rushing out without Nora's present. After three weeks away all she'd
got to place in that passive lap was the bunch of grapes
which Marty Pike had let her have cheap.

Not that Nora would know. She was too old
now – yes, and too daft, poor darling – to know much
at all. That wasn't the point. She, Eva, knew and was
ashamed.

But what a rogue he was, eh, Marty! She was over her
irritation now and could laugh about it. There she'd
stood, forgiving him yet again and thinking how it was
past history anyway and maybe no more than a temporary disturbance of the glands, when out he'd come
with the topless bit; and, after all that, to catch her up
halfway down the street and try to make a date to show
her the gravel pits! Would you credit the nerve of the
man? she asked Pussy, grinning. And looking me over
with those glistening eyes, the lecher, which is as near
as he's getting to my tan even though he did take
twenty pence off the grapes.

Eva always had to pause to brace herself before walking up the drive of the old people's home. She dreaded
this encounter – not the seeing of Nora, certainly not,

but the seeing of Nora here. Yet the place was incredibly well kept, there was no denying it; it was a credit to the Council – shaven lawns, bushes neat as pincushions, flowerbeds like vast, bright jellies. And where did they find the money in these hard times to keep everything just so? Not out of the maintenance budget, that was for sure. Rumour had it that they skimped on the food, but she'd dismissed that as typical Tigby gossip – for they couldn't, could they; not on their food, not the old people's? Still, she'd take a close look at Nora's lunch. Come to think of it, she hadn't dropped in at lunchtime for a long while. Since Alec left it was her evenings she'd spent with Nora.

But everyone agreed that it was a beautiful place – or, rather, a beautiful-looking place, or a beautiful-looking place if that happened to be your idea of beauty. It was perfection – though in a joyless kind of way, for couldn't a place be just that bit too polished to be home? Eva pondered it uneasily as she often did. Besides, with half the old dears blind and many of them dingo who was left to appreciate this meticulous order? And if it wasn't for them who was it for? To satisfy what?

Oh, *damn* forgetting Nora's present! She'd sent her a postcard every day, but that wasn't the same. Having found exactly the right shawl, she was looking forward to putting it round Nora's shoulders; and then, with all the time in the world, to forget! Well, back with us again later, she told Pussy, and to hell with the rule about over-stimulating the inmates.

Eva hurried up the drive. Geometrical gumdrops! Hard, obvious, regulated, constrained; put down in pots for limited growth, cleared out and done away with before untidiness set in – yes, like the people it was all supposed to be for.

Eva glanced back from the porch, thoughtful. It'd be bad enough for me, she confided to Pussy, and I'm young – well, you know what I mean, youngish, by comparison; young in spirit anyway. At least I could

43

fight back, make a joke of it, tell Matron to get stuffed. But imagine being past it! Imagine no one taking you seriously because you were old. Think of being trundled like a bag of washing between that geriatric museum in there and this raving mad garden, jollied along, patronised out of your dignity, popped on to a high-seated chair with a wipe-clean surface alongside another decaying body, though not for comfort, not for friendship, but – as I once heard a helper say – because it *looks* so much better when they sit in twos.

'Oh God, please let me keep my faculties!' Eva whispered, suddenly urgent and angry as though she'd just caught someone trying to filch them from her. 'Especially', she bargained, 'my bladder and my teeth!'

For if she ever had to put her teeth in a glass and didn't know or didn't care where she peed. . . .

She pressed the bell and saw her finger leave a smudge of mist on the polished brass.

She tried to imagine her own old age but could see nothing. And Alec? Would he die first or would she? Equally unreal the thought that either could die. Well, it would come, of course it would; but just so she didn't have to be a credit to the Council first – cleaned up and tidied away. Which, yes, Nora was.

It came to a head then, that accumulation of unease which had been with her for years. For hadn't she tidied Nora away the better to accommodate Alec? Guiltily, agreed; and protesting, yes; but she'd done it all the same because, in her despair, it had seemed the only way out. And, sharp-tongued though she often was, Nora had never reproached her for it. She'd given her a look sometimes which had made her uncomfortable, but not once had she put into words the bitterness she must have felt. Not once in nearly ten years.

Resignation? *Nora?* It was unthinkable. Yet what option had she given Nora but to be resigned?

'God!' Eva said aloud as the full realisation struck her.

But now things had changed. She had time to look

after Nora, and Alec would have to learn to accept that Nora was her – was their – responsibility. Perhaps she'd given in to Alec too much in the past.

'She's coming home,' Eva said. 'I'll take her back today.'

Her heart soared. There had been nothing to calculate, nothing to weigh. It was as though the decision had been lying fully formed on her tongue waiting only to be uttered.

She heard footsteps on the tiled hall floor, listened. That would be Bridie.

'How's the man Steve, then?' she asked, grinning, as the door opened.

'Oh, Miss Wootton!' The girl was startled. 'But. . . .' There was a certain embarrassment. Perhaps there was a new rule about lunchtime? 'I rather think. . . .'

'Isn't it convenient for me to . . .?'

'The way it is, Matron wants to see you. . . .' She stood aside. 'So if you'd ever wait in here, Miss Wootton. . . .'

Here being a wallpapered shoe box which smelt of Ronuk.

Yes, but how vexing about the kettle! There'd be no hiding the truth from Nora now, and she'd be really upset; for she never failed to ask how it was, her old kettle, and could still quote the occasion, even the date, when she'd given it to Eva. There was no confusion in her mind about the past, none at all; it was just which day it was today, or who was actually in the room.

More steps – this time authoritative ones, Matron's. Amazing woman, Matron. Plump, bonny, vigorous, unwrinkled – and all, or so she said, because of honey.

Eva smiled at Matron who was so full of honey and wholesomeness. Her 'Good afternoon' rang out warmly. But 'Good afternoon, Miss Wootton,' Matron said, reserved, cool, a little pinched. Like Marty Pike she seemed to be expecting more of her.

'I do hope. . . .'

'Come to my office, will you?' Matron cut in.

45

'Of course,' Eva said meekly; and she followed the discreet smell of lavender which accompanied all that health and authority to a larger box of a room which was also a-dazzle with polish. Not a book, not a paper, not a pin in sight. The curtains hung in rigidly parallel pleats. Three small pictures, their ears pegged back, stood shoulder to shoulder awaiting the firing squad.

'Sit down, please.'

A gesture to the upright chair facing her own across the desk.

'Thank you.'

Matron raised her brows. Clearly something had upset her. Mystified, Eva watched her arrange a little spray of words and fasten it with a twist of barbed wire.

'As you may imagine, Miss Wootton, I'm more than relieved to see you.'

'Relieved?' Eva's heart gave a bump. '*Relieved?*'

'She kept shouting for you – such an uproar! We had to increase her sedation. Understandable, mind you,' Matron said, chilly. 'You hadn't visited for a long, long time.'

'But I saw Nora the day I left! It was the last. . . .'

'You've been away?'

'Certainly.' Eva looked at her with astonishment. 'My holiday. . . .'

'Ah, but the old are like children; people should remember that. They become dependent, then feel abandoned if. . . . Unreasonable, but there it is. And it was extremely difficult for us, Miss Wootton, not being able to contact you when. . . .'

Blaming her, by God! Eva said sharply: 'But of course you could contact me! I left all relevant information – dates, addresses, phone numbers, flight numbers, times of flights, everything. Yes, and I left an authorisation with Nurse Baker for phone calls to be made to me on Nora – on Mrs Pringle's – behalf. I can't think what else you needed, Matron.'

'Then, it's a great pity it didn't occur to you to hand that information to me – as you'll appreciate, Miss

Wootton,' Matron snapped, going pink, 'when I tell you that I didn't even know you were on leave.'

'But Nurse Baker. . . .'

'Nurse Baker's left. She went a fortnight ago. Such selfish expectations, staff, these days. No sense of service.' She looked at Eva again, still cold, still puzzled. 'Well, at least we've cleared that misunderstanding up. And now, if you'll wait a moment,' Matron said, rising, 'I'll get your letter from the safe.'

'My letter? What letter's that?'

'The letter I told you about. The letter Mrs Pringle. . . .' She stopped. 'You did get *my* letter, of course? You must have done. It was delivered by hand because of the weekend.'

Eva shook her head.

'But Matron,' she said urgently, 'is she ill or something? I can see her, can't I? I. . . .'

'When did you get back?' Matron was asking.

'Early this morning.'

'Then my letter was waiting,' Matron said with certainty. 'I wrote it on Friday.'

'No. But what—?'

'Just a moment. Excuse me.'

Oh, but if this meant that Nora had been sent to hospital! How she'd hate that! How she'd resist! Please God, she prayed, not the hospital. I'll get her better without that – I can manage.

Matron returned, her neck mottled with anger. She said with some constraint: 'I'm sorry, Miss Wootton; I'm most sincerely sorry. My secretary should have made sure. . . . It's quite unforgivable. . . .'

'But is she actually in hospital? *Do tell me!*' Eva cried. 'You see, I promised her that. . . .'

Matron sat down again. For once she seemed at a loss, human.

'Miss Wootton,' she said helplessly, 'Mrs Pringle died on Friday.'

Eva gazed at her, trying to understand. But Nora couldn't be dead as Matron seemed to be trying to tell her. She was going to take Nora home today, if she was well enough.

'As you know,' Matron was saying, 'our rules don't normally allow. . . . But as we were unable to contact you and at that point didn't know there was a. . . . So it happened in one way as she would have wished, and I'm sure that will be a comfort to you in time to come. That she died here, in her own little room, I mean. And very peacefully at the end, very peacefully indeed. She knew nothing,' Matron assured Eva earnestly, 'ab-so-lutely nothing, my dear.'

'Nora. . . . But are you quite sure she's dead?' Eva stammered.

'I was with her at the end. I was there myself.'

'Nora?'

'Yes.'

'You mean she *is* dead?'

'I'm sorry.' Matron hesitated. 'And, of course, we've had to hand over. . . . As I told you in my letter, it was necessary to. . . . Oh, how much easier it is to say such things in a letter! Be assured, Miss Wootton, *I shall fire that secretary!* The cremation, by the way, takes place at ten past twelve tomorrow.'

'No!' Eva shouted. 'She isn't dead! I won't have it!'

And afloat on that polished linoleum lake in Matron's aseptic room she burst defiantly, untidily into tears.

Matron glanced at her watch, rang for a cup of tea, murmured that it was shock.

'Come, now, you've nothing to blame yourself for, Miss Wootton. You've been more than faithful over the years – and not even as though you were a relative,' she marvelled. 'Indeed, you've been far more faithful than many I could name who've let their own flesh and blood. . . .'

Matron did her best; but Eva had known Nora all her life and would not be so cheaply comforted. She'd felt closer to Nora, her adoptive mother's great friend, than she had to either of those wrapped-up-in-each-other people she called her parents and had early learnt to rely on Nora as, later, Nora had come to rely on her.

'Drink your tea up, my dear, and swallow this. It'll do you good.'

My dear. Like Marty Pike. What else was it that had reminded her of Marty Pike? She couldn't remember now; didn't, anyway, care. She wanted to think only of Nora, talk only of Nora; so she talked of Nora and that last strange dimension into which her mind had moved. She told Matron about the invisible man in the straw hat.

'But he wasn't invisible to her,' Eva explained through her tears. 'Nora could see him; and if he wasn't in the room she'd sit glancing at the clock, wondering aloud where he'd got to, worrying when it was foggy or grew late – you know how it is. . . .'

'Indeed, yes,' Matron said gravely. 'The brain can play very strange tricks.'

'No, she saw him.' Eva was stubborn. 'She saw him as clearly as I see you.'

For Nora did see the man in the straw hat. Eva was certain of it. She was instantly alert when he came into the room, reprimanding him sharply if he didn't take off his boater before settling down in the chair with the blue cushion which no one but he was allowed to use. How hard to explain this to Matron, though.

'He was real to her, you see,' she insisted. 'He was like the focus round which her life. . . .'

And she wept again, and bitterly, to think that that life was done.

But it was true. He was real. Nora would break off in mid-sentence to toss an 'And you know where you can put *that*, Ned!' into an apparently empty space. 'I will not have a gentleman covered in my house, and ye know it, ye divil!' Then, 'What a great baby he is, always trying to best me!' she'd whisper to Eva, but fondly, before smiling and nodding at the empty door-frame, the closed door, with a 'That's more like it; now you can make yourself at home. And ye know Evie,' she'd sometimes add. 'She needs no introduction, I'm sure.'

She, too, Eva, had got into the habit of nodding and smiling. At the shut door. At the vacant chair.

Just occasionally, if Nora had had a good night perhaps, or was talking more lucidly than usual, Eva would probe a little. Did Nora, in fact, see anything? Wasn't she just looking at a cushion on a chair?

Nora would sigh then, pitying her.

'Yes, Evie,' she'd say, 'I know the way it is, for haven't I heard often enough that because you can't see poor Ned he doesn't exist? Sure, I understand; it's only logical. But all the same' – examining the air above the blue cushion – 'ye're here as usual, aren't ye, Ned?' And 'There!' she'd cry. 'See that, Evie? If he isn't grinning at me, the wretch! Oh, where are your eyes, girl, that ye can't see what's before them!'

'That's how it was,' Eva said to Matron, mopping at those eyes, blowing her nose again, struggling to explain that Nora wasn't just any old woman, and about her grief and regret; and to do Matron justice she listened kindly and tried not to glance at her watch. 'I asked her once', Eva went on, 'why the man in the straw hat came to see her. And do you know what she said? "For company, of course. What else?" For company! Just like that, simple, as though it were the most obvious thing in the world! To please her, I said, yes, I understood; but she snapped back, "No, ye don't, ye stupid child! We were lovers, Ned and I, but that was a long time ago. Now he's waiting for me to be a girl again so that we can start life afresh and maybe make a better fist of things this time round." Wasn't it marvellous that she felt like that? Yes, and that she'd had a lover, bless her, and. . . .'

'Well, there are no ghosts in this house,' Matron said with a return to her brisk manner. 'And when you know as much about senescence as I do, Miss Wootton. . . .' She looked at her watch at last. 'Perhaps I'd better get your letter now; though there's no point', she added with a touch of chagrin, 'in giving you mine now, unless you. . . .'

Eva stood precipitately. Letter?

'Oh. Oh, yes, thank you. No. No, I don't. . . .'

'But that girl will go! You can be sure of that.'

Eva stood on, her mind a sudden blank, her eyes held by three pictures which were awaiting their own execution. Then she took the sealed envelope which Matron held out. Faded mauve. It would have a purple lining, and the paper inside smell rather chemically of violets. The times she'd irritably scoured the shops to find stationery like this, and the joy with which she'd do it now if it could bring Nora back.

'You're still shocked, Miss Wootton,' Matron explained, professionally kind. 'Have an early night and take a glass of hot milk with honey on retiring. Remember, Mrs Pringle died very peacefully, very peacefully indeed. *She knew nothing – whatever – about it,*' Matron added, as though this was the last word to be said on death.

Her name was written on the envelope, *Miss E. Wootton*, in Nora's bold and earlier hand.

'Thank you,' Eva said helplessly as she followed Matron out through the door to the tear-dazzled drive, the letter tightly clutched against her side.

7

Nora, Alec. . . .

It had been wrong of her perhaps – had it? – but at the time what else could she do?

She stared at the sky which was silvered like the lining of an oyster-shell. To the west striations of pink, of peach, like those dreadful dresses. Above them, charcoal strokes presaged the oncoming dark.

What else could she have done? There had been no problem in Garchester: in those early, tentative days there was no reason why Nora and Alec should meet. But once she'd committed herself, bought this house; once Nora had moved in, as she had every right to expect to do. . . .

It was a miracle, come to think of it, that they'd even managed to spend that first Christmas on their own.

Nora arrived in the New Year and by mid-January the trouble had already begun. Who's this Alec always hanging about acting as though he owned the place? Burroughs? *Burroughs*, did ye say? Sure, wasn't that the man you were secretary to in Garchester, the feller with the wife's photograph stuck in the middle of his desk – I remember ye laughing about it and how they all tried to have a bigger one than the next? So what's he doing here, Evie? Has he followed you or have you followed him? Jesus, Mary and holy St Joseph, girl, what are ye thinking of! A married man? Have ye no sense! And 'Ah!' Nora cried in a frenzy of regret, 'so that's why ye didn't snap up that great chance in London! And ye'll not get another like that this side the grave! Ye great soft eejut! My heart's scalded thinking of you . . .!'

And so on, and so on.

If only Nora had made some effort to hide her jealousy. If only Alec hadn't sulked when Nora was around. If only Nora hadn't delighted in being around in order to make him sulk. If only Alec could have laughed them off, those innocently-delivered observations with venom in the tail. But it was impossible. She was torn apart between them – hence the Keepsake Home, reputedly the best of its kind in Tigby.

At least she had insisted on what she believed to be the best; but she felt shabby now to recall that it was Alec who had pulled strings so that Nora could jump the queue.

And now death had solved her problem, and she was bereft. Nora dead! The fact was totally foreseeable, totally unforeseen – yet another fact which had erupted to confound her, something else she should have taken into account. And that death – had it been the happy release Matron implied? Who could tell? And, if it hadn't, who was to know that, either? Certainly not Matron, whose prayer was for ignorance at the last. For doubts were messy as grief and growth were messy; a torn conscience, a sense of sin, the ravages of the Holy Spirit – messy, messy, messy! Let's sedate them!

But what if Nora hadn't died in induced peace? What if she'd died in disorderly distress, in a muddle of pain and fear, disoriented, calling for Evie who had deserted her – what then? Which was preferable, that, or an end so chillingly and with such easy words referred to as increased sedation?

Flaming, dulling, quenched, the light had died. Eva turned stiffly from the window, switched on the lamp and began to undress. Glimpsing the telephone, she froze for a moment, willing it to ring. If only he'd ring, if only he'd write! Or if she could get in touch, spill out her misery, hear his voice. But she'd promised not to until he gave the word and, no, she wouldn't break her promise. Yet how hard it was, this waiting. Their pact entombed her.

She remembered then – Nora's letter! – and half into her nightdress scrambled towards the door, for she'd left her old white handbag hanging in the hall. Then she stopped, for she was, she found, deeply reluctant to face those stairs, that waiting silence and the stillness beyond her door. Half-ashamed, she turned the key and stood, heart thumping, drawing the familiarity of the shut room round her like a cloak, promising herself that tomorrow, yes, first thing, she'd read what darling Nora had to say.

Tomorrow. What was she going to do with tomorrow when it came? And her own death – what of that? How amazing that the most important day of one's life should come unannounced. To think that once a week she stubbed her toe on the day of her death and once a year on its date – but which date, which day? What a comfort it would be to know! Like 'Market day, eh? Awkward as usual, Eva!' or 'All Saints? What splendid casting!' But to come in ignorance, live in ignorance, go in ignorance. . . .

Given the choice, though, would she choose to slip away in a sludge of sleep or would she have the courage to face her angel?

She turned over, pulled the pillow more closely under her cheek.

But not to know, just not to know. . . .

After a while she got out of bed and opened the curtains. Darkness like a bottomless hole stretched up from the pallid street-lights. Eva shivered and went back to bed, lay staring at her thoughts.

'Oh, go to sleep!' she counselled Pussy at last. 'Take a sleeping pill, can't you!'

But, no, she couldn't. They were in the bathroom, and tonight she was afraid of the dark.

If only she could have stayed asleep!

In the end, against expectation, she'd plummeted, gone fathoms down. Then, yeasty, gaseous, an inner unease had grown, inflating itself within her and drawing her with itself, bubble-like, to consciousness – plop!

Wide awake now, heart hammering, anxious, she watched the lights from a passing car pare her walls. A clock chimed – All Saints again. Eva checked the strokes on her fingers. Eleven. Twelve hours ago, a lifetime ago, it had struck eleven then. Oh my God, was it still only Monday?

It was still only Monday.

This time last night she'd been on the plane with the gang – Not long now, chaps; let's have another drink! – revving up for the last goodbyes. Mind you gimme a call. Do write, dear, won't you? And drop in any time you're passing; just take us as you find us, eh?

And Latchy: 'I'll miss you, Eve. Keep in touch.'

Only twenty-four hours ago. And Nora already dead. Nora dead – the last thing she'd thought of.

So what had she thought of? Alec chiefly; and getting home to read his letter, that letter which was going to put everything right, that letter which hadn't yet come.

Well, better not think of that. Or not now. She was tired enough already. Weary. Weary to the bone, to the marrow of the bone; and she must look ninety at least, ninety, with dull and nested eyes, that golden-girl tan no more than sallow flesh. Pitiful, embarrassing, to the young disgusting even.

She winced, recalling Harry's stare.

Yes, she was weary; but how wide awake, too, that exhausted body. Wakeful aching arms, wakeful aching hands; a longing to give, no one to give to – did Alec ever think of this?

Alec. Why, in that high-minded moment, had she encouraged him to go away when everything in her screamed to keep him here? In an attempt to share his ambition? To prove she wasn't petty? Because she

55

trusted him? Because she didn't trust him? Because she was a great soft eejut?

Eva turned her face to the wall. Stop it. Go to sleep. But, drained, flayed, glaring with exhaustion behind the hot sockets of her eyes, her brain, independent of will, shuffled and endlessly reshuffled that much-fumbled pack of cards, her life – all the cards, it now seemed, jokers.

Harry's face was still before her, grey, fungoid, with dead, contemptuous eyes. Past it. That was their verdict. Past it.

Was she, then, to everybody a figure of fun, pathetic? Eva plunged over, back to wall, face to window, her lids clamped against the rising tears. But this wouldn't do – by God, it wouldn't do! Not self-pity. Not that cheapest sweetie of them all.

She began to recite, got stuck at 'Return, Alphaeus, the dread voice is past/ That. . . .'

' "That"?' she said querulously. 'What comes after "that", Pussy?'

It was hopeless. She was twitching with wakefulness. Stretching her legs, she searched for a patch of cool sheet, a position which might ease them, but found only staleness and a burden of covers. Her feet, hands, felt like overstuffed sausages and niggled with an indefinable ache. Wretched without, sickened within – for she'd identified it now, that ugly disquiet which had wrested her from sleep. Those awful women!

'No!'

Eva snapped on the light and, almost panting with disgust, pulled her wrap round her shoulders. She couldn't, wouldn't, lie here thinking about them. She wrestled with her door – why on earth had she locked her door? – then went padding down to make a cup of tea.

She should never have gone to see the body.

At once she corrected herself. That wasn't what she meant, of course it wasn't. It was right to have seen Nora. She was glad she'd seen Nora. She had been awed, uplifted, by the startling beauty that body had achieved in death. Eyes sealed like cockle shells, like the great untroubled lids of a foetus, all vulgarity quenched, the runaway girl from the Dublin slums – fine-boned, marmoreal now – had been accepted into the enigma, become an aristocrat in stone.

It wasn't the dead, no, it was the living who had offended – if, that is, they were living and not some subtler form of death. Whisper, whisper – she'd smelt it at once, that stench of words, and waited for the clustering bluebottles. But there were no bluebottles, only two smooth slabs of fat and shoulderblade filling the scooped necks of two summer dresses like obscene ice-creams.

Even from the back of the bus on her way from the mortuary chapel, wiping her eyes yet again – she died without me, poor Nora; and did she even understand why I wasn't there? – then sighing, trying to adjust herself, for Nora was out of reach of hurt now, and putting on lipstick and generally preparing to come back into the present once again: even from the back of the bus and preoccupied as she was she could tell what they were up to, those women, gouging away Tigby-style at some poor devil's reputation, relishing the destruction, savouring the filth, circling like the missing flies, yearning towards it, shit that it was, drawn to worship and feed. Even half a bus's length away from those scoops of porcine flesh in the pink and peach polyester, even though she turned her face resolutely to the street – as at first she did – blinking through her tears at the glare outside, trying to concentrate her thoughts on something worthy, even so the dirt was with her. She couldn't shut it out, that base antiphony – It happened so and so/No! Go on! Did it really?/As true as I'm sitting here. . . . /She never did!/She did./She did?

'Which, Pussy, is the trouble with dirt: it draws one to it.'

For when that first voice dropped again in revelation

Eva had felt an urgent need to know – true or not – what had been done which should not have been done, and when and by whom; so, pretending – yes, to herself – that she wanted to be out of the sun, she'd moved into the seat behind the two women. So that she could hear better. Pitiful, Pussy, pitiful!

Well, she'd heard better all right; and, engrossed, the women had noticed nothing.

'Well, it couldn't have been easier, could it? I mean, being next door she had it. . . .' (Pink Dress.)

'Right. Yeah, right. She'd set it up for herself, I can see that.' (Peach; the jackal.)

'And her gentleman friend. . . .'

'Married?'

'They always are, the ones that sort goes for.'

'Right. They always are.'

'And dropping in at all hours, as good as living there – well, you can guess. The neighbours did. Not many secrets there, eh? But this time I'm telling you about. . . .'

There was a prolonged screech of brakes. Eva missed the next exchange. Pink Dress took up again.

'. . . And my husband reckoned it'd been going on for months, if not longer.'

'You don't mean with the . . .? *All four of them?*'

'No doubt in Jay's mind. It really upset him. I never knew Jay so upset except over the boy. But she was the guiding light. Brazen – that's what he called her, brazen.'

'*Well!*' A release of breath. 'I should think he was upset! I'd have been upset, walking into that, that. . . . *Disgusting!* Any decent man'd. . . .'

'Well, with a woman like that at the centre of it what can you . . .? But he took the opportunity to drop a hint to the gentleman friend. Met him at some function or other and. . . . On the q.t., of course. Tactful. Just let him know which side his bread was buttered. Hinted that the lady was *persona non grata* and that if he wanted to get on. . . .'

'*Persona non grata!*' marvelled Peach.

'A likeable fellow, apparently. Very affable, Jay said, with a good career ahead of him. Got into her clutches, I suppose – you know what men are: it can happen to the best. . . .'

'Right, yeah, I know what men are. . . .'

'Anyway, Jay spoke to him man to man; friendly. Willing to let bygones be bygones, give a helping hand. . . . Never bore malice, did Jay. . . .'

'Salt of the earth, men like your Jay was. . . . But what about the others?'

'Others? Oh, still there; though they haven't exactly got a fan club, I hear. There have been some pretty heavy hints by all accounts.'

'And do you think they . . .?'

Peach shoulder crowded closer – whisper, whisper. Pink shoulder shrugged.

'Do leopards change their spots?'

'Right, do leopards . . .? And they're cunning, of course, people like that are. I wouldn't be surprised if they hadn't burrowed. To keep it dark, I mean. That's what they'll have done, you mark my words, burrowed.'

'Burrowed?'

'Through the attics. They're semis up there, aren't they? Well, there you are. It's what happened in Railway Terrace with the Pakis, isn't it? They say you can walk from end to end under the roof and find them sleeping like sardines. . . .'

Pink Dress was a-jelly with laughter. Whisper, whisper, whisper, then a yelp from Peach.

'No! Was it? Was it really?'

'As true as I'm sitting here.'

'Many a true word spoken in. . . .'

'And what's more. . . .'

'*She never did!*'

Voices lower now. Gurgles like water in a partially stopped-up drain. More dirt, more degradation – and she, Eva, had chosen to listen – chosen to. Had moved nearer so that she could.

On her feet, trembling with distaste, she tapped the women on the shoulder.

They both jumped, startled, as Bob had been: and, though she said nothing – for when it came to it she was too upset to speak – her mute contempt was surprisingly effective. Frozen in a salacious confidence, elbow raised to nudge, they gaped back at her like a pair of appalled codfish; and, head high, Eva got off the bus and walked home.

She tried to dismiss the memory, but it was still with her. Soiling, vaguely menacing, it lay undigested on her spirits like a sour dinner.

Poor devils, anyway, whoever they were, those Tigby victims.

The kitchen clock said ten to one. Monday was over at last. Sleepless, Eva sat on in the kitchen which still smelt of charred enamel, poor Nora's kettle which. . . .

Nora's letter!

The dull shell of her mood cracked, heaviness fell away and, although tears started again, she was joyous. She had resisted the urge to rip it open, that mauve envelope, devour the contents then and there in the street, jostled by God knows whom; for to have it here, at home, in peace, to glance from it to Nora's old bedroom curtains now cut down for the kitchen, then back to those scented pages – Nora's idea of luxury – wasn't that what she would have wished? Wasn't it what she wished herself?

'Darling, *darling* . . .!'

Eva wept and laughed together as she lifted her old white handbag from the hook in the hall.

8

No birds yet in the blackberry dark where silence stretched like a taut wire. Birds? There was no letter, either. Wallet, yes, and yesterday's shopping list; but the mauve envelope was missing.

She remembered taking it out so that she could feel it in her hand. She must, she supposed, have put it in her lap when she felt for her lipstick. And then, of course, she'd walked further up the bus. . . .

Of course. The better to hear the dirt.

She hadn't gone back to bed. What was the point? She wasn't likely to sleep now.

But would she ever get it back, that letter? There was nothing she could do about it, nothing she could do until morning except regret.

'You make me ashamed,' Eva said aloud.

She got up to sniff the curtains, Nora's curtains, which still held the acrid smell of burn, fingered them sadly. Threadbare. They'd never stand up to a wash. And that would be another link gone.

Across the kitchen she caught sight of Doris's letter, recalled her childish vow.

'Oh, but darling,' she explained to Nora, 'I didn't mean you!'

Eva opened the window, and the coming day thrust cold hands against her face. She shut it, touched the curtains again. She'd have to replace them soon. She put on a saucepan of water to heat. Made yet more tea.

A quarter to four – not bad, not bad. A day was on

its way in and that meant it was on its way out, which was the way for days to go.

'Alec. . . .'

It was a long time since she'd heard herself say that in the early morning, a long time since he'd been there in the early morning. She smiled, waiting for it.

'Mmm?'

Reluctant. Prodded out of him. He did so hate to be woken up, poor Alec.

She thought then about how she loved him and the way he was. Well, she told Pussy, who wants a plaster saint?

A cock crew like a thin neon scribble peaking on the dark. She put out her hand – tap-tap – to see if the teapot was still hot. It was Alec's gesture – tap-tap.

But was he such a very ordinary person? Timid, Nora had insisted; certainly nothing to write home about.

Oh, but that letter! If *only* she hadn't. . . . But she had, and that was the end of it. There was nothing she could do till the bus office opened at nine.

Timid? She could have said weak; she could have said vain; she could have said he was sometimes obtuse – what of it? It would all have been true, all have been false. It didn't add up to Alec. Anyway, what did it matter? What had love got to do with deserving? She loved him because he was Alec, because she was Eva. Was that how God saw people, like a lover?

She stared at the papers in her hand. Without meaning to, she'd slit the envelope of what Doris chose to call an epistle, only there wasn't an epistle this time, just a mass of information – cookery classes, Greek for beginners, yoga – and a scrawled note: *Welcome home, strangler!* . . . Startled, Eva peered again at Doris's florid script. Ah. *Welcome home, stranger! I trust this finds you in the pink as it ought to after all that galli- vanting. Did you have a lovely time, lucky old you? Enclosed now out of date but to set you thinking about the autumn!! No time like the present, can't have you moping. I bet you didn't get your bus pass – typical! Will pop in soon to stir you up, Aye, Doris. P.S. I want to hear all about it. Were there ANY CHAPS??!*

Chaps? Eva sighed and dropped the papers into the bin.

'Sorry,' she said aloud to Alec, 'I didn't mean to. . . .'

She felt as shifty as though she'd broken their pact.

But what an extraordinary thing it was to love someone. And what reasonable woman would ask for more than the love of the man she was fond of? Yes, however ordinary – whatever 'ordinary' meant. And no doubt Jean Burroughs felt the same. Why not? It was disagreeable, perhaps, but it was understandable: she could feel for Jean in this.

Where she could not feel for Jean, what she could not understand were those phone calls – and no, she told Pussy, she never would.

Jean's telephone calls began a few weeks after Nora arrived. They weren't angry calls; they weren't hurt or threatening – nothing like that; they weren't even frightening, not in themselves, though her guilt made them so. No, they were light-hearted, amiable, usually spur-of-the moment – Just two minutes, then I must dash – that kind of thing: but always with an invitation to tea, to drop in for a drink, see a film, take an hour off for a pub lunch.

And why? So that they could get acquainted. For she'd heard so much about Eva, Jean – his wife – had said.

Yes, indeed, they would have to get acquainted – and bitterly, no doubt, when Jean knew the truth – but that was a different thing. Alec hadn't yet spoken to Jean about a divorce.

The first time it happened she was terrified. Nora, fortunately, was out. Alec came in to find her sitting white-faced on the stairs; and at the sight of him, not even kissed, she cried out: 'She knows!'

'What?' Alec smelt her fear though he missed her words. His mouth was suddenly not quite his own, oddly stiff. 'What is it?' the rigid lips asked. 'Not the Chief . . .?'

His panic augmented hers. She whispered: 'Your wife. . . .'

'Jean?' Quickly: 'What about her?'

'She phoned.'

'And the message?' (Mouth still moving woodenly.)

'No, no. . . . She phoned,' Eva said fearfully, 'to speak to *me.*'

Astonished, she saw the puppet mask relax into a face again. Relief steamed off him.

'Oh, really?' he said in polite surprise.

He couldn't have understood.

'Me, Alec, me! She wanted to talk to *me!* It was awful!'

'Awful?' His voice was sharp now. 'What do you mean, awful?'

Eva whispered: 'She invited me to tea on Friday.'

'But she didn't leave any kind of message for me?'

'She didn't ring the office, she rang me here, at home; that's what I'm trying to. . . .'

'Oh.' He was looking at her, apparently still puzzled. 'Then, what did Jean say that's upset you so?'

'Oh God, what didn't she say! Would I go to tea, and if not tea, then for drinks, and preferably Friday. Because she wants to put a face to a name. . . . Alec, she knows my name! And she let drop that she knew I was with you in Garchester . . .!'

'Eva, darling, listen, you silly girl, *of course* she knows your name and that you were at Garchester! You *have* got yourself into a state about nothing!'

'But, Alec . . .!'

He pulled her up from where she crouched, a rigid huddle near the front door; did his best to cradle her stiff body, press her head against his shoulder, tousle her hair.

'Here, come on, now; you had me scared! I thought at the very least the cops were after me. Or that that old fool Salwart had choked himself on his policy and manpower reappraisal. And what about a kiss, eh, since we seem to be alone tonight . . .?'

'But, Alec, your *wife* . . .!'

His wife had rung her at home and he was actually inviting her to laugh! She struggled against him, unmollified.

'Listen, love – no, listen; do be sensible. Jean rang to invite you to tea – that's what you said, isn't it? To tea, please note, or for a drink – right? Not to a drama, not to a showdown, not to an eye-scratching-out contest, to tea.'

She said reluctantly: 'Yes.'

'Very well, then, what's so awful about being invited to tea? Accept.'

'*Accept?*'

'Why not? I'll run you out, of course, drive you back. . . .'

She was outraged. 'How can you even begin to . . .?'

'I repeat, why not? Karen Lawrence came to tea in Garchester; Helena Brewer – no, you didn't know her, but she came to tea, too; and Winnie Smart's been – so why not Eva Wootton?'

'Why not me? Alec. . . .'

'Oh, come on! Whatever you haven't picked up about Jean, you must at least know by now that she's incurably hospitable. After all, you do keep my diary.'

For no reason she could precisely identify Eva was offended, and at two levels. Above all, she was affronted by what seemed to be his amorality. Yet at once she became confused. She was knowingly the mistress of a married man. What right had she to these fine feelings concerning his lack of moral scruples? And so, all right, what if she did keep his diary? It was part of her job, nothing to do with her private life.

She watched, silent, as Alec took off his raincoat. The heavy hanger, his, was the shape of a splayed wishbone. His fingers found it, unhooked it, slipped it under the shoulders of his coat, hung it up again; and all the time he smiled at her as though this were any normal day. He seemed to have no inkling of how she felt. Went prattling on about his wife. As if she wanted to hear about his wife, let alone meet his wife. As if she could bear to. Not till they'd sorted things out, not till Jean knew the truth and they could meet as the adversaries they were. She'd have the courage of a lion then. But now, in this diminishing no man's land. . . .

'. . . And such a friendly girl,' Alec was saying. 'You're bound to like her – everyone does; she's such enormous fun. Lively, outgoing, sympathetic. . . .'

It burst from her, and she winced as – too late – she caught the shrewish note. 'Would you like me to take down your wife's reference in shorthand, *Mister* Burroughs?'

He looked as startled as though she'd slapped his face.

'I was only trying to explain why Jean phoned you.'

Eva studied him, troubled.

'You don't mean you really do want me to accept that invitation?'

'Yes.'

As simple as that – yes.

'But, Alec, seriously – come to your home? Meet your wife? Me?'

'I'd like it.'

Simple again. Direct. Still smiling.

'But, Alec, the implications . . .!'

'Darling, I just don't see what you're fussing about. You'll get on famously with Jean.'

'*I don't want to get on famously with your bloody wife!*'

Vast amusement from Alec then – ho-ho-ho! Incredulous joy.

'Love, you're jealous! I don't believe it!'

'Of course I'm jealous, you idiot!'

'But you've nothing to be jealous about! You know I adore the. . . .'

'Oh, haven't I!' But grin, Eva; keep back the tears. 'I could scratch her rotten eyes out!'

'Don't do that, darling; they're pretty eyes. Besides, she darns my socks.'

'Aha, now we're getting the truth at last! It's the man's socks that he's. . . .'

66

Grinning still when she'd rather have wept – that, or scratched in earnest. Out, vile jelly! His.

Later, she said cautiously: 'Alec. . . .'

'Yes, love?'

She turned to look at him.

'I got the impression that Jean had guessed.'

'Guessed?'

'About us.' Watching him. 'That we're lovers.'

Oh, nudge, nudge! For an intelligent man how thick he could be!

'What gave you that impression?'

She was certain of it, absolutely certain; but she said uncertainly: 'I'm not sure I can explain. Something in her voice. But I felt it; I definitely felt it. . . .'

'Felt? Felt?' Indulgently. 'Fanciful woman!'

'All the same, Alec. . . .'

'What is it now?'

'Jean hasn't guessed, has she?'

He appeared to weigh the question.

'Guessed? No, she hasn't guessed.'

'You're sure?'

'Yes, I'm sure. She's guessed nothing.'

Eva sighed. The real question, surely, wasn't whether Jean had guessed but when she was to be told. And once again she'd lost her nerve, shrunk from asking.

'No,' she said at last, 'she'd hardly invite me to tea if she'd guessed, I suppose. I must have been wrong.'

'So you'll change your mind, love?' Holding her tightly. 'You'll come on Friday?'

'How can I? No, I'd feel cheap, awful, sort of treacherous.'

She already felt all three. And did he never feel cheap, awful, treacherous when with the wife who, apparently, hadn't guessed? That's what she really wanted to know. Or did she? On balance it might be preferable not to know a thing like that.

Eva touched the teapot again – tap-tap – but it was cold now. She got stiffly to her feet and walked to the

67

window. The sky had paled to a sullen grey with, to the east, shrill notes of light which looked so metallic, thin, that they seemed to squeak as they scored the gloom. Any moment the first blackbird would whistle.

She turned to face Pussy with it.

'I'd have known!' she said with conviction. 'Catch me not knowing she was his mistress, that Eva, if I'd been his wife! Of course I'd have known. How could one not know a thing like that?'

And she imagined such knowledge like a knot in the web of the marriage she and Alec might have had, a snarled thread which the finger of love and custom would unerringly find – yes, however veiled the deception, however competent the lies.

But how it had hurt – and still did hurt and give offence though it had long since ceased to threaten her – that he should have wanted her to meet his wife, and in their home. So that he could imagine her there, he said, when she wasn't; could look at where she had been and take comfort from it. Besides – though more tentatively said, this, but not tentatively enough said which should never have been said at all – think of how much more often they'd be able to see each other, he and she, if only across Jean's drawing room.

And that was another thing – *Jean's* drawing room? When she'd agreed to go with Alec to Tigby it had been understood – she thought it had been understood – that as soon as possible it would be her, Eva's, drawing room. For that she had tossed aside her own bright future preferring what, to her, was the brighter one of being at his side. That had never been in doubt in Garchester. That had been their agreement surely, her right?

Right? She recoiled from the word. She had no rights. Rights were a matter of contract, of law. Jean had the rights. But what were rights worth if love no longer invested them, and she, Eva, had that love. It was her certainty, the firm ground on which she stood, that Alec was the man alongside whom she should grow. For this she could violate her conscience – was violating her conscience – and for this she would joyously take from his hand when he held it out to her that second-rate gift, those stolen technicalities, rights.

How could she, then, meet Jean until Jean knew her for what she was? Not just the name to which, politely, she now wanted to add a face. Not as efficient Miss Wootton who kept her husband's diary, cleaned the spots off his tie after a canteen lunch and got him and his papers to their meeting on time; but as the equal for whom her husband was leaving her, the thief in the court of love.

After a few months – three? four? – the phone calls had stopped and Jean Burroughs had never tried to contact her again. She'd held out and she'd won. Even Alec, in the end, had accepted the fact of her unmovable obstinacy.

Yes, but. . . .

She'd missed the first whistle. It was in full flood now, the clamour from the garden, jostling, vibrant, predatory; a joyous impulse to the daylight coupled with an impulse to take, to keep, to kill. Eva rested her face on her hands. Yawns as big as boilers, no stopping them. Worn-out little screwed-up eyes, OAP eyes. Oh dear, oh dear, oh dear!

Yes, but Jean had still not been told and sooner or later she'd have to know. Eva nerved herself to say it at last.

'So why not, darling, now? Give me one good reason. . . .'

It was strangling, humiliating. She died a thousand deaths; was, above all, hurt that it should be she who was forced into taking the initiative. But it was true. This *nothing* couldn't go on. Jean would have to be told. So she got them out somehow, those words. Dropped them into his silence. Waited.

It took all her courage. For to seem to force, to extort from him. . . . The idea was obscene! She valued only what was freely given, what he wanted to give her – like his love.

All the same, she said it again, pleading with his averted face.

'We can't go on like this, Alec. It isn't fair to any of us.'

'I know.'

When he looked at her at last she saw that his eyes were moist.

Arms don't calculate. They're made to be used as shields and welcomes, arms. Hers were round him now.

'Darling, what is it? What's wrong?'

How could he tell her? He couldn't even begin.

How could he not tell her, she demanded stoutly. What sort of woman did he think she was – made of sugar? If something was wrong, then they'd share it, find a way through together – it was insulting of him to think she wouldn't understand! 'So all right, Mister,' she told him, holding him close, 'tell the old girl. Out with it!'

He came out with it.

'Eva, I've got two children. . . . Darling, how *can* I leave them till they're grown?'

Children? Alec? She'd never even guessed. Found she couldn't speak. Sat back on her heels and looked at him across the wreckage.

'Say you understand!' he cried, terrified.

In a dead voice, at last: 'Yes. Yes, I understand.'

How desperately he'd loved her then – tender, passionate, afraid. She mustn't leave him! He hadn't told her before because. . . . Would she swear not to leave him? He needed her so!

Leave him? How could she leave him? Hurt or not, deceived or not, she was committed. Whatever it was she was now committed to.

A wife? It was brutal thinking, but she'd steeled herself to think brutally: a wife could be set aside. Children, though – young children, Alec's – she had no armour against them, those children of his. How could

70

she be instrumental in making him give them up?

Back at the window she stared out into the tin-coloured light. She thought of the desert she'd glimpsed from the plane – where? In imagination she saw it now, wave-ribbed and desolate like the fossil of some arid sea.

9

Dry-eyed, ill at ease, Eva stood in the noonday glare
outside the crematorium chapel. There was no shade
anywhere. The driver of the hearse mopped his neck.
Her flowers lay limp on the lid of the coffin, expiring
too. She felt somehow raw, unfinished, crude, an
affront to the occasion.

Occasion? Meaning the disposal of a wooden box?
Eva glanced at it without emotion. Nora? No. Impossible to take in that Nora was there, that this was the
end. It was unreal.

Her discomfort, though, her unease, the trivia of
the occasion, they were real enough. The heat beat
down on her black felt hat turning her head to a
sweating pudding. Her hands were too big, too heavy,
too hot, an itching burden in their cotton gloves;
her feet swollen and old beyond their years; and in
this stifling dark dress, too tight under the armpits,
wrinkled across the back, she felt cheap, ugly, unsuit-
able.

She eased her weight from one foot to the other as
the gravel knuckled up against the thin soles of her
best black shoes. Averted her eyes from somebody
else's box. Caught the eye of Nora's driver. Looked
away again. Found nowhere else to look. And oh, she
fretted, examining the fastenings of her odious gloves,
pretending to make them more secure, what an afflic-
tion it is to be a woman alone in a public place! And
yes, she thought, compassionate, I'm sure that's why
they have gigolos, those sad, rich old women. I don't

believe it's just sex – no, I don't – not when your feet ache and there's no disguising the fact that your hair's too thin and your jowl too thick and that what you really want is a nice cup of tea and a good night's sleep. But to have someone to appear in public with, someone whose arm you can lean on, someone you can hand over to, smile at, touch; someone with whom you can exchange a look; someone good-tempered who'll fetch and carry, run your errands; someone to hide your vulnerability behind. . . .

Eva started. A hand was on her elbow. And wasn't it a lovely day again? Matron was saying – voice muted, though, as befitted a funeral; almost apologetic, it seemed, for the sunny weather.

Good morning, good morning. . . . Or is it good afternoon?

A round of exchanges. Eva had expected to be the only mourner; but here was Matron, soberly summery, a credit, as always, to any occasion, accompanied by Frank Knapp, Nora's solicitor, and a dark-suited elderly man whose face she knew well but couldn't place.

But the sight of Frank Knapp jolted her. Someone else – Matron? Knapp himself? – had reasonably enough gone ahead with the funeral arrangements in her absence, dealt with the immediate practicalities of death. The bills, though, the clearing-up – that responsibility was hers; and, shocked, she realised that she hadn't thought of it till now.

She began abruptly: 'Mr Knapp, could I have a quick word . . .?' But, excusing himself to the others, he was already drawing her aside.

'I'll pay the bills, of course,' she told him, plunging in. 'Would you see that I get them? And I'm so grateful for all . . . to whoever. . . . I couldn't have been away at a worse time, could I? As for the – you know, the clearing-up and all that . . . I presume Matron'll be getting in touch. I'll have a word. . . .'

'Bills, Miss Wootton? You mean for the funeral?'

'Yes. And yours, too, of course, Mr Knapp. And anything else outstanding. . . .'

'Oh, you needn't worry about those. The estate'll cover everything like that. Indeed, arrangements were made. . . . I'll be writing to you about the estate – Mrs Pringle's will, and so on – within the week.'

'Estate? *Nora?*'

He said drily: 'Yes. Mrs Pringle sprung one or two little surprises on us, didn't she? I presume, by the way, that you got her letter? The one left in Mrs MacDonald's care?'

'Oh, Matron. . . . Yes.' Eva blushed. 'Or, rather, the awful thing is . . .'

The clerk at the bus office thought they might recover her letter. The cleaners, he told her, were very careful and all lost property, however trivial, was supposed to be handed in. Not to do so could cost the finder his job – or her job, the clerk had added quickly. Yes, by all means call back; but if she'd leave her address. . . .

She'd done both; but the letter had not yet been recovered. She'd left her address; had had to be satisfied with that.

'The awful thing, Mr Knapp . . .' she said urgently.

But Frank Knapp's eyes were on the stranger.

'That's Sean Feenan, as you must have guessed – Mrs Pringle's relative.' He glanced curiously at Eva. 'Perhaps we ought. . . .'

As she must have guessed? Eva followed him. Sean Feenan? She'd never heard of Sean Feenan. In all the years she'd known Nora, which was all her life, she'd never heard her speak of any family except that disastrous husband of hers. So what relative was this?

The dark-suited man was watching her, and now he raised his hat and looked her frankly in the eye. Eva stared back, her brows wrinkled, suspicious, on her guard. She had met him. She was certain of it now. But who was he?

Frank Knapp seemed about to introduce them, but after a glance at Eva's face he changed his mind.

'We're running late' – he examined his watch – 'which isn't unusual on market day, I've noticed. Tigby needs a bypass; I've been saying so for years.'

Matron agreed. 'Though myself,' she said, 'I'm not convinced that to take a road through Bixteth. . . .'

'Preferable, surely, to demolishing. . . .'

'Good morning,' he said, looking at her expectantly.

He was even smiling, this man who had appeared out of the blue to pay his last respects to Nora to whom, astonishingly, he seemed to be related; and perplexed, troubled – for how *awful* to have lost Nora's letter, and how foolish to know a face so well and yet be unable to place it – and, yes, how confess a thing like that without giving deep offence? – Eva in her guilt and confusion frowned where, normally, she would have grinned a welcome – to the fishmonger, to the dustman, to anybody let alone Nora's relative.

The man's smile went. He turned abruptly and walked away. At once Knapp joined him and they stood together ostensibly studying the rose-bushes.

'Oh!' Eva said under her breath, stabbed. She hadn't meant. . . . Of course she hadn't! And she was about to follow him, try to put things right, when Matron touched her arm.

'At last! High time, too. Come along, Miss Wootton.'

There was a sudden stir of activity round the chapel. The doors were open now, and mourners from the previous funeral dribbled out. Eva watched as the waiting coffin with its pathetic wilting flowers was drawn from the hearse. Nora was in that box. It was true. This was goodbye.

Matron gathered up Frank Knapp and the relative, and she would have gathered Eva, too, into her tidily-organised party had Eva not shrugged away. But desolation had smitten her at last. Nora was dead – she could believe it now, and that this was the end, intolerable. Separating herself from the others, her face

75

averted, Eva sought a seat in the farthest corner so that she could weep alone.

When it was all over, by the time she'd wiped her eyes, said another prayer, forced her hands back into those hideous, those respectful gloves, Matron and her party had gone.

10

In spite of the heat and her thin tight shoes Eva decided to walk home; for she could not, no, really, she could not with her lids puffy and her nose red and in this welter of misery and rage, the memory of yesterday's harpies still with her, bring herself to face the eyeing crowd of a Tigby bus.

Nora. That she should be dead was one thing and bad enough; but that she should be done away with like that. . . .

Tears welled again. In time no doubt she'd come to accept the fact of Nora's death. But the squalor of Nora's going, the crudeness, ineptitude, vulgarity – never! She felt violated.

She huddled for a moment against the window of a television rental shop to mask her weeping from the passers-by. Inside, a smooth face filled a dozen screens in cloned consort; then a tide of words rolled over them, a twitch of groups erupted. Eva moved on.

She regretted the walk now. She was urgent to be home where she could kick off her red-hot shoes and feel the kitchen floor cool against her feet as she made a cup of tea and tried, as well as she could, to come to terms with the deep offence of Nora's going.

For offence – that's what it was. And oh, no flowers, she mourned. Think of it, no flowers! Only her own little bunch drooping on the coffin, wounding her by its cheapness. And what of those rituals which should have honoured Nora at the last, adding a dimension in keeping with the dignity of death?

'What of them? You may well ask!' Eva told the old woman in the unbecoming black hat who, pig-eyed from weeping, paused to glare back at her from a shop-door mirror.

Because what words were there to describe the nastiness of it all? That baby-doll drawing room they called a chapel. The boudoir lighting, easiglide curtains, the musical treacle which came oozing from the walls. She'd half-expected to see a card displayed: IDEAL HOME. CREDIT TERMS AVAILABLE.

And no one – herself, yes, but no one else, not even Matron – knew the words of 'Abide with Me'. Certainly that young parson didn't – that is, if he was a parson and not a sales rep done up in clericals to humour the customers. She couldn't sing in tune, no; but, by God, she'd sung! Cheeks scarlet, head high, she'd belted out every verse of Nora's favourite hymn and to hell with the lot of them! For Nora had taken to hymns once she'd given up religion.

And then the nerve, the bloody *nerve* of the man not to have got his facts right! How dare he, that priest, stand up and thank God for Nora's life as wife and mother – Nora who'd broken with Tom Pringle after three weeks of a marriage which had never been consummated! She didn't know much about Nora's brief excursion into wedlock but she did know that, for Nora had boasted of it; and as she listened, outraged, she'd imagined Nora listening, too, and could almost hear her cackling laugh echoing round the hereafter, for though Eva was wounded by it it was Nora's kind of joke. Was it the relative's kind, too? she wondered.

Eva glanced down at her feet, one hobbling slowly after the other along the iron-hard paving-slabs.

Oh, but why hadn't someone – why hadn't she – stopped this obscenity in its tracks? Why hadn't she risen up in the wrath she felt, torn back that box from those crooningly-closing curtains and borne it away to bury it decently in the soil with love and flowers and history?

Her tears had dried leaving the skin of her face tight and sticky. She longed for hot water, for a chance to release her mutilated feet, her throbbing head, pass a comb through that sweat-plastered hair. For coolness, comfort – and, God, yes, a drink. Perhaps that above all, a drink – and how well Nora would have understood.

Oh, but the drink did her good. Well-being began to pulse back. That was better. She felt more like Eva again, so down the hatch and damn the price.

She'd ordered brandy, the best, a double; sardonic, had watched herself ordering it as Nora would have done – daring old girl! Sparky OAP! If only Nora had been there to add her own rasping comment.

She sighed, looked about her. What was this place called? The Royal Derby? It figured. The bar had recently been done up to resemble stables, the waiters were dressed as jockeys. Pity we don't know any of the hosses, she told Pussy.

For how good it would have been to see a friendly face. Or if the relative had walked in. She felt she could cope with him now, the relative; would even dare to tell him she'd forgotten who he was and say wasn't it awful of her not to have remembered where they'd met and that the name Sean Feenan rang no bell and that she hadn't known he had any connection with Nora anyway. Why, they'd put things right in no time, soon be laughing about it over another drink.

The jockey stood before her, tray tilted like a quoit.

'Anything further, madam?'

'The same again, please.'

She smiled at him. Nice boy. He looked a bit depressed, though. Saddle-sore?

She was floating a little above it, that grey ache which occupied the gap where her consciousness of a living, breathing Nora had once been. She could look down with compassion on the space, not quite objectively, not yet, but feeling a little rosier than she knew she was. Which was all to the good. Balance? she asked

Pussy vaguely. Whatever it was, Nora would have approved.

She drank to the concept, looked round the room again. To be straight with you, Pussy, I'd be glad to see anybody at the moment – Moo, Archie, even Doris. . . . Well, no, but almost anybody, la Hampstead, of course, excepted. Not that there was any fear of running into Lorraine these days, thank God; not since she'd netted that marvellous job, wherever it was, and was about to marry – maybe already had married? – the love of her life.

To think that there had been a time when she'd tortured herself sick because she thought Lorraine Hampstead was after Alec!

She could look at the whole thing quietly now, or very nearly; but it had been a bad patch. She wasn't herself then, not at all. Racked by suspicion, building double meanings into everything he, Alec, said; misinterpreting, apparently, everything she, Eva, saw; mad with jealousy. . . .

She pulled herself up. Cliché. Sorry, Idris.

But could one be mad with jealousy? *Mad?* She thought about it, drained her glass. Yes, cliché or not, one could. She had been.

'The same again. . . .'

Reckless, Eva, reckless! She shook her mane at herself.

Mad, yes, that's what it was; for out of all proportion, the devouring violence of that jealousy. And then to deduce from what Angela said that it was without foundation! Yet it could have wrecked everything. Her relationship with Alec could easily have foundered on that pettiness of hers. And she still felt petty – why not admit it? What a burden was lifted when Lorraine left! Not to run the risk of their paths crossing and be obliged, for decency's sake, to say good morning. Yes, and not to have to look at the commonplace little bitch and marvel at her beauty.

'The game asame. . . .'

Dignified now, the right hand disdaining to know

what the left hand was drinking. Medicinal, though, brandy, she told Pussy. It prolonged life. Or so she'd heard. Which wasn't a thought to be dismissed lightly, not after a funeral.

Yes, it was madness, nothing else; for to have suffered such anguish, lived through such a nightmare, and for no more than a fantasy, wasn't that mad? Such a cliché of a fantasy, too! Ageing woman, sweet young flesh, tempted lover – classic!

We must remember we're prone to them, she told Pussy, fantasies.

But they seemed to be wanting to shut. She worked her feet back into their shoes, fumbling for her wallet; then the door opened on to a pavement as blinding as any of those beaches – oh, oh! Balanced high on her legs, Eva set off towards it, shading her eyes.

'Whoops!' she cried, clutching his arm.

One shouldn't wear such tight shoes, really one shouldn't, she confided to the gentleman who steadied her, but they were black, you see, suitable for a funeral.

'Not at all,' the gentleman said.

Not at all? She didn't follow. But he was a fine-looking man, though ageing – as Latchy was ageing, as Alec soon would be – with a bald spot on the crown like Alec's. And yes, indeed, she agreed, smiling at him, it was a lovely day. Pardon? Oh, no, sorry, she had an engagement – but thank you so much.

Pardon? A revolting expression, her so-called mother's expression: she'd thought she'd left such niceties behind in her adoptive parents' house. And to pretend it was her shoes when she knew perfectly well it was the brandy walking – she ought to be ashamed.

Still nodding her thanks Eva hurried off down the street, her feet miraculously their right size again, ready for the fray. Whatever that was. Fray? *Fray?*

The word took on a life of its own and went bouncing from wall to wall across her skull while she stood apart and watched herself, a woman with a calm face like a figure in history, only drunk.

She'd stuffed the change from a ten-pound note into the pocket of her dress. She stopped to count it. To count it a second time. Oh dear.

You'd better start remembering you're an OAP, she told herself, though without acrimony. As Bob would say, live and let live. Suddenly she found it very funny.

Had he realised she was an OAP, though, that fellow back there with time on his hands and a look in his eye? She betted herself he hadn't.

She thought about it. Sighed. No, it wouldn't do.

'Now, what do I mean by that?' she asked Pussy, startled. The feeling which came with the words was minatory.

Ah! She'd placed it: it was that person she'd called Mother again. Then 'Oh, you poor child!' she whispered, looking back across the years at the child who was herself; looking back, too, at the woman who, half a century before, had asked her to hold her baby.

She could see the woman still – yes, and far more clearly than she could recall Gwen, whom she'd been with only three days before – and the voice, unforgettable, was more precise on her ear than Latchy's.

'Just for the minute only, sweetheart,' the woman had begged. 'I have to pick up a bag of groceries, d'ye see, and that stuffy old shop's no place for a baby.'

Eva had longed to nurse the baby but, tangled in dread, had refused. Because it wouldn't do. She wasn't ever to speak to strangers or reply if they spoke to her – that's what Mother had said. Because it wouldn't do.

The woman had been incredulous. 'And aren't ye an unfeeling child!' she'd shouted after her down the street. And 'What were you thinking of, girl?' her mother had cried when the story came tumbling out. 'A decent poor woman, and with a bairn? Of course I didn't mean that! Where are your wits? I meant' – and she lowered her voice – 'gentlemen.'

Gentlemen? Then why hadn't she said so? Eva wept

afresh. It seems she could have nursed that baby – apparently had done wrong not to hold the baby – and now it was too late.

What baggage we carry with us, she marvelled, what dreary baggage. For why should she, who'd forgotten so much and dumped so many and heavier burdens, be unable, after fifty years, to rid herself of that vivid grief?

Nora alone had understood, had tried to comfort her and wept with her when she failed. But Nora usually did understand. She'd understood everything except Alec.

Nora's letter – would she ever get it back? And, oh, the Johnsons! I forgot to go round, Pussy. Where, indeed, are my wits?

11

Coke cans, sweet wrappers, cigarette packets – the usual litter had been tossed over the wall and, as usual, left there. She'd cleared it up herself before now, out of sheer irritation; but it didn't bother anyone else into action, least of all the cleaners. A bit of coping had been knocked from the corner. Whose car this time? She glanced at Mr Salwart's space, but it was empty. Of course. Tuesday. Area Joint Committee.

'Oh!'

Eva felt herself blush. Out of old habit she'd walked to County Hall; had hurried, even, as though returning to work after too extended a lunch-hour. Already she was halfway across the car park.

It was bad enough to have come back at all – she hadn't intended to – but to return precipitately in the middle of the afternoon in unbecoming black clothes, her handbag bulging with hat, and no make-up, no fresh shampoo and set, no time to compose her face for the occasion, no radiant holiday snaps. . . .

And now, damn, Bert Elliot had seen her. He was holding the door open, waving her in. She put her fingers to her hair, willing herself to look smaller than she felt in that tight dress.

He touched her arm.

'Sorry to read about the old lady, Eva. Not a bad innings, though, was it?'

Read? She hadn't thought of that, either, the announcement. Who had? Matron? Frank Knapp? Or had the mystery relative arrived in time to take charge? She felt a spurt of proprietorial resentment and was immediately ashamed.

'I just wish I'd been home. . . .'

'I know. Anyway, come on in.'

Diffidently, she stepped over the threshold, felt awkward as she glanced about her.

'Well,' Bert said more briskly, 'it's good to see you – and quite a surprise, I might add. I thought when you last stormed out you'd shaken off the dust of your feet for good; instead of which, here you are back to taunt us.'

She switched on the bright smile of a woman of leisure who has just acquired an expensive tan, switched it off again. She needn't bother, not with Bert. But just look at the place! Just look at it, she told Pussy.

She was trying to keep her eyes from the red poster warning the public not to leave parcels unattended. Since she'd left it had been torn and the tear cobbled with a twist of Sellotape; and someone had scrawled a phone number across a corner. There was a stack of such notices – new, unmutilated – in the front office, main desk, bottom left-hand drawer, and they all knew it; then wouldn't you think, she fretted, that one of them might have summoned up the energy to get a replacement!

Bert was examining a thumbnail as though its presence was a mystery to him.

'So you're enjoying life?' he remarked, biting the quick then thrusting his hand into his overall pocket. 'That's right. A tour, wasn't it? Nice for some.'

'As one retired person to another,' Eva countered, 'are *you* enjoying life?'

'Relishing it, Eva. They say water finds its own level and I've found it – assistant doorman. But I don't take life as seriously as you do, which is a great help when times are hard.'

Elliot had previously been a principal lecturer at a college of education, one of many to be closed because of a diminished need for teachers as a result of falling rolls. When, in his mid-fifties, he was made redundant he took what was supposed to be a temporary job – hanging about in the hall, as he put it, keeping out all the nuts except those who were paid to be there. No one knew how he'd managed to get the job in the first place or how he kept it – it was his boast that he'd bribed his way back to work – but he insisted that he'd never been so fulfilled in his life.

Eva hesitated; then she asked, for she couldn't resist it: 'What's going on these days?'

If anyone knew, Elliot would. The staff swore that the Chief consulted him when he wanted to find out what was happening in his own office.

'It gets worse and worse.' Elliot beamed at her. 'It's insane. I love it. It'd drive you crazy. I reckon you got out just in time,' he told her. 'Here, come and take a look at this.'

Eva had always liked Peter Elliot whom, nowadays, she had to remember to call Bert. Bert, he said, encapsulated the image he was anxious to promote, this being the day of the common man. When it suited him he had a voice to go with the name.

'Take a look at what?'

'Something which may startle well but not astound.'

'Milton?' she hazarded, pleased.

'Right.'

They'd first met when she'd gone with Alec some years before to take notes for the minutes of a meeting at the college of education. It had turned out to be a meeting of paralysing boredom, atrociously chaired. Catching her eye, Peter had slid a note in front of her: *Has this fellow no feeling of his business?*

Hamlet's voice in the middle of so much tedium! They'd been friends ever since. He was a slight, fine-boned man with lively eyes and narrow face, the kind she thought of as Plantagenet; and, like Latchy, he was a man with whom she could be at ease. She found herself glad, after all, that she'd come.

86

'I'm a bit tight, Bert,' she confessed. 'I drank too much after the funeral.'

'You could have fooled me. I thought it was lavender water.'

'No, that's Matron.'

'Well, my duck, it takes all sorts.' He glanced at her. 'Want a cup of tea?' he asked in his normal voice.

'No, no. . . .'

He led the way across a small carpeted area set about with potted cacti and a few selected pieces of woodwork and embroidery from local schools. The display hadn't been changed since before her holiday; nor, apparently, dusted.

As though he read her thoughts, Elliot said: 'Job demarcation lines, Eva. Assistant doormen don't dust.'

She retorted with spirit: 'No, and secretaries aren't supposed to clean up outside County Hall but. . . .'

'But you go looking for trouble and I don't.'

'OK,' she said, resigned. 'You've got a point, actually.'

They walked up the back stairs into what, three weeks before, had still been the Treasurers Department. Here, a glazed gallery overlooked the well of the central hall, an area used as front office and resources room. It was a place of much coming and going, the hub of their small universe; and, glancing down, Eva was struck by the air of mechanical absorption with which her old colleagues moved. It was as though each followed a pre-ordained path which, in isolation, he or she was pro-grammed to cover. Perhaps a word processor wouldn't, after all, be out of place.

She paused and, turning back, Elliot joined her. Derek Walton drifted into sight, a file in one hand, a cigarette in the other. He left the file by Benny, who went on typing in pointed dismissal, shoulders hunched. Yawning, he wandered off in the direction of the lavatories, the cigarette between his lips, his hand already feeling for the paperback in his jacket pocket.

Edith Bardwell shot across from Staffing, appearing as he disappeared. Leaving the door to swing behind her, she began manic operations at the photocopier, glancing up fretfully when Martin Thornhill, apparently shouting, ran towards her waving his diary. And all this while Dotty Kingston went leisurely through the post, popping each letter daintily into its pigeon-hole as though feeding chocolates to a poodle.

Eva had seen it all before and so many times; it had been reasonable then, the way life was, but how meaningless those apparently purposeful actions seemed to the outsider she had now become.

Outsider? Perhaps 'convalescent' was more appropriate.

'Like to drop in on the old gang?' Peter, Bert, was asking.

'Gang?' she exclaimed, startled, disoriented.

'Sites and Build—'

'Oh, no! Good God, no!' She tugged at her dress. 'Some other time,' she added, feeling she'd been churlish.

They turned together and walked on.

'Filthy, isn't it, Eva? But there have been problems.'

'A strange feeling, though, seeing it all empty.'

'Yes. The Clerks and Treasurers moved last week – they're the lucky ones; they've got beautiful suites. Especially the computer. He's got the best suite of all. Other sections, as you may or may not know, have fallen on harder times.'

'Really?' Eva was interested. She could recall the original plans well. Alec used to bring them to the house and they'd spent hours, days, poring over them on her dining-room table, brief to hand, notebook open, pencil poised. 'But provision was made. . . .'

Elliot smiled at her fondly.

'I love the language – *provision was made*. Yes, and so it was; I saw the old plans, too. Like the kingdom of heaven it was going to be, many mansions, even if you did get soaking wet going from one to another with the mail. Well, it's been redrawn any number of times since then and shrunk a bit in the process; not to mention that the aesthetics have been tinkered with – a little less of the Frank Lloyd Wrights, if you understand me, and more overtones of cake-tin.'

'But at least the building's properly finished?' she asked.

'That depends on what you mean by properly and finished. It's been *declared open* – oh, yes – and by the highest in the realm who could be persuaded to soil his hands by having anything to do with the squalid affair. But it isn't ready for human occupation – or, if they think it's ready, it isn't fit for it. Not as planned, or as some of us were led to believe was planned. I can't give you a definitive list of defects at what our friend Peter O'Pan will insist on calling this moment in time because we're still at the teething-troubles stage, meaning there's a fresh revelation of horror every day. But they did, for instance, put the main staircase in back to front; and very humorous it looked, very humorous indeed. Gave those in the know a lot of innocent pleasure until they ripped it out and started again – which is more than they can do with the sewage disposal system.'

'With the . . .?'

'Well, you know the way it is,' Elliot said indulgently. 'There was this chap looking for somewhere to put a manhole, so when he found a nice empty space on the plans he drew one in. Only it wasn't an empty space; it was the staff canteen larder which Polly hadn't got round to detailing, and when she did it was on a different copy and somehow the two never got married up. So now, apart from tearing the building down, there's nothing they can do except not use the larder. It's under what they call discussion at the moment, with memos flying hither and yon, not to mention tears and accusations. The powers that be, of course, don't want to spend any more money, so they're trying to persuade Polly Arkwright that she doesn't need a larder. In fact a top-level directive's gone out, copies to God knows who not, decreeing that larders aren't forward-looking any more and hinting that it was time Polly started preparing herself to come into the twenty-first century, which is the battle-cry of that load of hooligans the ratepayers have just voted into office. But Polly isn't taking it lying down; and I've seen some nasty yapping little notes of a practical nature from Polly asking where she's supposed to put her bulk buys. It was you christened New County Hall Salwart's Folly, wasn't it, Eva? Well, awe-inspiringly true it's turned out to be. On top of which it no longer includes everybody under the same roof – though that, I seem to recall, was the whole purpose of the exercise. . . .'

Elliot stopped and flung open a door.

'There you are. Have a good look,' he invited.

'Good God!' Eva said, shaken.

It was the old Committee Room; now, apparently, in use as a store. Lengths of carpet stood on end, lashed into giant Swiss rolls. Chairs were stacked into the semblance of some Heath Robinson machine, a tangle of interlocking legs and backs with, here and there, a cushion hanging drunkenly by its tapes. Desks were on top of tables, on top of one another, on top of anything which would support them, however tenuously, and a trampoline stood on one corner among them like an angular ballerina on her points. Books were parcelled with string, hundreds of books, some escaping to buckle and splash into whatever space was available; and as for paper, there was paper everywhere – slithering from overloaded tea-chests, leaking from cartons, from carrier bags, from split packages, from cupboards which had burst their locks, from the interstices of filing cabinets. Every flat and horizontal surface – all that was flat was by no means horizontal – was crowded with objects which would go nowhere else: half a dozen sewing machines, a truss of football boots, some boxes of new tennis balls, rolls of ageing posters held together by elastic bands, a tray of mugs and an electric kettle, a faded green baize notice-board, a videocassette recorder, some bales of fabric, a jam-jar full of hog's-hair brushes and a box of tins of powder colour, a pair of gumboots tied carefully to a garden spade and labelled *O'Hodgkinson* and, under the nearest table of all, a sack from which spilled dirty sand. In the centre, high on a cupboard which was on another cupboard, beyond hope of reach, was a microwave oven topped by a baby's bath.

'Good God!' Eva repeated. 'Is it a jumble sale?' She glanced into the nearest tea chest. On top lay two dolls, one explicitly male, the other female and in an advanced state of pregnancy. She examined the tag labels: *Human Relationships Programme. Return to J.O'D.* 'Or a sex shop?' she hazarded.

'You shock me,' said Elliot. 'Those are educational aids. But isn't it a picture? They've had to come in here because the advisers' rooms have already been gutted so that they can be made fit for temporary occupation by the Careers people. On the other hand, Staffing's been promised this accommodation till it can move to the new building. Its own is being taken over by Playing Fields on Monday and there's a bad hiccup on the new site; which means that Staffing could be here for the next three months and wants this clobber out sharpish – and would you blame them! Which in turn means that the advisers should be the next to go; but the trouble is there's nowhere for them to go *to*, poor sods, the reason for which is obscure and interesting as well as depending on whose side you're on. There's some say nobody remembered we had any advisers so they weren't included in the brief, and hard luck; and there's others say there was a secret plan to axe advisers once the cuts began to bite, and to avoid delay when this came to pass the plans were redrawn behind locked doors by those in the know – only when the advisers' union put a stop to that little caper nobody remembered to tell the architects that it was back to the drawing board, boys. Here, Eva, do you ever get the feeling you've seen it all before?'

'But Peter, Bert . . . if the advisers aren't going to the new building and can't stay here . . .?'

'Ah. Yes. An interesting one, that; Sam's running a book on it. The rumour that's being given the most credence by the ones who ought to know is that they're to be divided between that condemned fish and chip shop the Council's just acquired because of the value of the site and the chapel the Methodists sold off cheap last June. Anyway, there it is. It has been ordained that the advisers shall go forth; and since transport's been laid on for Monday morning go forth they must. But there are complications like – as I said – nobody knows where they're to go forth to, or, if he does, he hasn't told anybody else – least of all the advisers, who are in piteous disarray. Bill's had enough of it and has very sensibly applied for early retirement. But the others are too young to get enhancement if they go, so there are some high-minded words on the subject of solidarity being bandied about – that is when they're speaking to each other at all. Oh, we've a right case-history of conflict on our hands, I can tell you. Make a good subject, it would, for one of those sabbaticals all the failing members of the profession seem to be getting in this time of financial restraint. Aggie's on tranquillisers and Ern's hitting the bottle so hard that Heads are beginning to get maiden-auntish about the way he smells. As for Peter O'Pan, he doesn't get out of bed at all now, except for emergencies – or so I hear. They call it working from home. Yes, and I could even bring myself to be sorry for the rotten layabout because, in spite of what their union says, the prospect's none too rosy, not the way I read it. What I read is writing on the wall, you mark my words. . . .'

'Oh, come on, Bert! Surely they can't. . . .'

'Can't?'

'Security. . . .'

'Security? With a change of party and the particular red herring this one's flourishing I reckon it could be off with the frills and back to basics before you could say vox populi, vox dei twice. And not, I might add, without support from central government. It was all over the *Argus* while you were away. Councillor Pike, for one, has made some very stirring speeches about the value of the three R's. He wants to get back to them, he says; they're England's heritage. But we all know what Councillor Pike means by the three R's – slate pencils, fifty to a class and no talking in school. There's a nice little row going on at the moment with the Curriculum Development people – to name but a few. The great cry, as I expect you know, is accountability – no wonder Aggie's swallowing tranquillisers by the handful! – and along comes Councillor Pike. . . .'

'Councillor Pike? Who's he? One of the new lot I. . . .'

'Who's he? Why, Marty Pike, of course! And done very nicely, too. Don't tell me you didn't know he was Leader of the Council?'

'Marty Pike? I don't believe it,' Eva said flatly.

'You'd better. This is a democracy – or hadn't you noticed?'

'You mean Marty Pike *actually got in?*'

'Romped home, the cunning bugger. And you can't say he didn't work for it, Eva.'

'But that ridiculous manifesto about swords and bucklers . . .!'

'Don't be snobbish. This is the age of the common man, and he's a child of our time is Marty. Vicious. Which makes him a true representative of the people who took the trouble to get up off their backsides and go out to vote for him, *which* – or so I've been led to believe – is what democracy is all about.'

'Oh, but Peter, really! I mean, Marty Pike . . .!'

'Yes, that sod.' Elliot gave her a sidelong look. 'Things aren't gentlemanly any more, Eva.' He hesitated. 'Listen, we're old friends, right? Then, I'm going to talk to you straight. Stop underestimating Marty Pike. I know you don't like him – I've heard you say so more than once in your usual refreshingly forthright and unguarded fashion, and I dare say you've cause.

But so have other people heard you and they may hold different views – so watch it, eh? He's dangerous, is Marty, in his spiteful little way; and now he's got power. He could', Elliot said, picking his words, 'bestow some useful favours. . . .'

She said with spirit: 'We all know scum rises to the top!'

Elliot sighed.

'There you go again! All I'm suggesting is that you should use your head for once. Because you ought to get a job of sorts, Eva. You'd find it helped; and I don't just mean with the money. . . .' He shook his head. 'I worry about you sometimes. Why did you leave like that, not a squeak out of you except for a few rather straight words of a personal nature, or so I heard, when NALGO would have twisted the Authority's arm . . .?'

Eva said stiffly: 'It was a matter of conscience.'

'Conscience! That's what I mean. It's a matter of mobs, my girl, and mobs are about power; because forget fancy names like workforce and management. . . . Well, you'll get used to it in the end, but I still think you ought to find something to do.'

'I'm fine!'

'Oh, sure,' he said, 'you're fine.'

There was a silence. He wandered across to glance down into the well of the hall again, turned back. He looked her over affectionately.

'God, Eva, I miss you! There isn't a soul left in this place capable of a civilised literary aside. I've often wondered why. . . . Well, no business of mine, of course, but it would have been more you to read Eng. Lit. than spend your life taking down memos about provision being made and unforeseen eventualities necessitating.'

She said quickly – too quickly; odd how painful it could still be: 'Look who's talking, you with your first-class hon. . . .'

'There is no virtue like necessity. I quote.'

'Richard the Tooth?'

'Act one, scene three,' he said unsmiling. 'A useful

speech, I've found. Worth rereading when you've nothing better to occupy yourself with.'

There was another silence.

'Well . . .' she began, glancing at her watch.

'Don't go yet; I want to talk to you.' He stretched up and disentangled two chairs. 'Ah, there's Mabel; I'll get us some tea.'

'Not for me. I. . . .'

'All right.' He sat down facing her. 'Mr Burroughs', he said abruptly, 'was here for the official opening last week.'

'Mr . . .?'

'Your old boss, A.C.G.B. himself.'

'*Alec?*' She felt suddenly unreal. Alec had been here, then, in Tigby? 'And how was he?' she managed to ask.

'He seemed all right to me – perhaps a bit thicker-set than before. The North suits him,' Elliot said without looking at her. 'Feathered his nest quite nicely, too, by all accounts. Mind you, he always did know how to take care of himself did A.C.G.B.'

Did he? Were they talking about the same man, about Alec? And that he'd been here last week?

Mabel came clattering near. Bert took two mugs from the advisers' tray and got them filled. He put one in her hand.

'Anyway, Eva, he asked me to tell you, if you looked in, that he sent his very best wishes for your retirement. In fact he said he was only sorry you weren't still around so that he could convey them to you personally.' She said nothing. 'Those were his actual words: "convey them to you personally".'

'Oh. Yes. I see.'

'I gather it was a bit of a last-minute decision. Coming to Tigby, I mean, for the opening.'

'Oh,' Eva said again.

Elliot sipped his tea, examined the mug. '*Cyanide,*' he read. 'Well, many a true word spoken in. . . .'

She smiled vaguely, wondering what she was agreeing to.

'A thoughtful person, Mr Burroughs,' Bert said with sudden ferocity. 'Quite the ladies' man. Asked after all the girls. Even remembered that mousy little thing who used to be in the front office before Gwynneth – what was her name? Chris? That's it, Chris.' He kicked out at the nearest tea-chest. 'You knew he was divorced, of course?'

Eva held her mug (*Grandpa*) close to her face between cupped hands, eyes lowered. Would she die on a Tuesday, then? Had she consciously stubbed her foot against the day of her death at last?

'Eva. . . .'

Do nothing, say nothing. Just breathe in, breathe out – no more's required of you.

Elliot got up. After a while he was close to her again, had taken the mug. Eva straightened her back and looked about her. It was still Tuesday, still daylight. She and Peter were in the old Treasurers' section staring in on advisory chaos. Nothing had changed except that Alec, apparently, was divorced.

She couldn't remember standing but she found herself in the corridor with Elliot at her side. A figure bustled across the floor below them, briefcase in hand. She recalled the label on his stacked pending tray: L.T.B.W.

'Let the buggers wait? I thought so,' Elliot said. 'As always, our hearts beat as one. And that's the man', he marvelled, 'who divided the sum in excess of estimates by the number of pages in the brief and struck the same amount off each page regardless. Very tidy it looked, too, scrupulously egalitarian; but it did result in some rather bizarre decisions when translated into bricks and mortar. . . .'

He put his arms briefly round her, held her tight.

'And now, Eva my dear, I'm going to call a taxi and either take or send you home. You've got to learn to be tough. Remember what I said about mobs. You mustn't let things wound you so – work, I mean, of course, you daft ha'p'orth.'

12

She heard a wondering voice say, 'Alec . . .' and the street bulged like blown glass.

Fists at her eyes then. You dare, Eva Wootton! Look out of the window, concentrate, get home.

A dazzle of sun-glazed road unreeled on the yellow afternoon. There was a swirl of buildings on a corner, then a screech of brakes as the traffic jammed suddenly like wedged candy bars. Stuck outside a cut-price store. Let the buggers wait. She focused on the windows which were scabbed with black and orange screams – FOUR PEE OFF! SEVEN PEE! *FREE GIFTS!*

Free gifts? Some gifts not free, then, Idris? It seemed not.

A viridian dress swept into a red phone box. Pinkness stepped off the kerb – pink skirt, face as fresh as a fondant, strawberry hair piled in abundance, a blouse as bright as seaside rock. Then an arpeggio of feet, a skein of movement as three children scampered by.

Three children – three? But there were only two who couldn't be left, Alec's. Alec who loved her, who hadn't written, who'd been in Tigby a week ago, who was now divorced – what kind of sense did that make?

She made straight for the brandy swathed in a slip in her suitcase. The room was still in appalling disarray made worse by the things she'd tossed from the shelves in her last-minute search for the funeral hat.

Eva held the bottle high. It seemed important to

make clear to herself precisely what she was doing. Drinking. And too early. Right, so she was drinking – drinking again – and too early. For the mind must not be left free to speculate, not yet; nor – worse – for the feelings to blossom. Not till she'd had a drink, two drinks, two large drinks, if need be the whole bloody bottle. And, even then, where was she to start? Where on that long road was there a starting point for the task of trying to understand, for the terrifying task of making sense out of chaos?

But having borne the bottle with such defiant ceremony to the kitchen Eva hesitated. She weighed it in her hand, then put it carefully down, dead centre, on the table.

'Actually, I don't want a drink; what I want is to have *had* a drink. . . .'

Well, that or for the telephone to ring. Alec, joyous, with explanations which, like a rising tide, would flush her from the shallows.

Back in the hall she stood gazing at the stairs. Those stairs where she'd waited for Alec.

'What I need now is to get the facts straight. Yes, the facts.'

Eva marvelled at the reasonable words which came out of her. Then, without apparent transition, she found herself in the kitchen blinking under the harsh glare of the ceiling light – but switched on by whom when dusk had begun to swill the house? She looked from the broken seal on the bottle to the glass in her hand, to the more than generous measure.

'Oh, and I didn't mean to drink . . .!'

But greedy like the starlings who haunted her lawn she gobbled it down, topped up again.

'That's better, Pussy.'

Cool, her mind's eye followed the graph of the drink's ingestion. All the same, she hadn't meant to drink. She'd thought it out, decided not to, and now she was. It was disgraceful. The puritan uppermost, she looked haughtily away while fingers still deft unscrewed to add another meagre capful.

'Right. That's your treat and you've had it!' The voice of that adoptive mother again smudging pleasure by dismissing it too soon. 'Now get a move on, my girl, and do something useful for your keep!'

Eyes owlish with drink and wisdom, Eva looked about her. For something to do, something useful. For, yes, that's what she must do. Something. And useful.

'Alec. . . .' She backed away from the sound. 'No! No, I won't. . . .'

And there she was again where, so long ago, she'd waited to confront him with her all-is-lost face. That's where she'd sat, on the third tread. The same carpet, even. Nothing changed.

Nothing? Had that monstrous fact made no difference, then – that Alec was divorced and hadn't bothered to let her know?

A voice cried: 'I won't! I can't! Not yet!' A calmer voice said: 'Slippers.'

So up she toiled once more, once more negotiated the obstacle race of random objects, unwashed clothes. It was like part of a dream landscape, as were her slippers neatly aligned on the dressing table, filling the round glass tray, echoing back at her from the mirror.

Slippers? Who wanted slippers? She'd lie down.

With trembling hands, mumbling and groaning, she peeled off the hot, the knife-edged tights, tore at the suffocating dress, the constricting slip, the bra which bit so unkindly into her soft flesh, the boned girdle constraining that plump round belly which so craved to be free.

'Just for the minute only, sweetheart,' she told Pussy, stabbed again to tears.

Eva woke up shivering. For some reason the duvet was underneath her. She had to drag at it, tear it free, before she could hutch her body in its comforting glow.

The wind had got up while she slept. She heard it

whisk at the curtains and rattle the bills which she'd thrust under the lump of driftwood. She liked to hear the wind.

Warmth crept through her, an osmosis of ease, a promise of yet more sleep. Then she lurched, for there was an ambivalence in that comfort. What had she forgotten – to put her room to rights, pay her bills?

A little light leaked in from the street lamp. Not yet asleep, not quite awake, she lay and watched through half-shut lids the fluttering rise and fall of those greyed papers restrained by the driftwood.

She knew the driftwood as well as she knew her own face, and her eyes closed on its image. Dense, impacted, a fragment of oak which some long-ago tide had taken and tumbled, rolling it like a marble in a game. It was oil-smooth now, bleached, luminous, beautiful like bunched fingers. She'd found it one day abandoned on the driftline. . . .

Alec!

She tried to fend it off again, but this time the pain would have none of her and came flooding in until she thought she'd drown in those harsh waters. Remote, as from a stranger, she heard the cries. But unmistakably hers the cheeks wet with her own scalding tears. Unmistakably hers that information. Unmistakably her own. *So* sorry he hadn't seen her – to Peter, Bert, the doorman, to be passed on next time she happened to look in. If she happened to look in.

And what if she hadn't looked in? She hadn't intended to go back; had, in fact, decided quite positively not to go back, it was all too painful. She'd gone back out of no more than old habit – that, and the drink – and so happened to get those good wishes of his. What the hell was she supposed to think good wishes like that were worth!

'Damn you, Alec . . .!'

Couldn't he, for God's sake, have phoned? Yes, yes, they had this agreement, but a divorce changed everything. Like their lives.

Their lives? His was changed, yes; but what about

hers? Ugly with tears, hideous with hurt, 'Well,' she asked, 'what about me, Mister Burroughs? You remember me, Eva?'

Like an engine starting up, something within her began to throb, gain momentum.

'How dare you! How bloody well *dare* you . . .!' Light on, duvet tossed back, she was out of bed to confront him with it. 'Now, let's have the truth!'

For it was, after all, Peter who'd told her about the divorce. That little item hadn't been part of the good-will package. So far as Alec knew, she could still be in the dark. But she wasn't in the dark. She had him cornered.

'Well, Mister Burroughs . . .?'

It broke over her again like a wave. Alec and Jean were divorced, and she'd heard the news by chance from the doorman!

It was she who'd been the strong one last year when, tentatively, he'd spoken of a job in the North, promotion which was apparently his for the asking; but she'd seen how badly he wanted it, that job – and he was ambitious, Alec, he enjoyed power. How could she stand in his way? Besides, time would pass; and with the children almost grown. . . . Give the younger one a few more months, he'd said.

In any case, he was going to tell Jean. That was a firm promise. He couldn't go on as things were. It was just a matter now of choosing the best moment – well, she could see that, and that this moment was private to himself and Jean. Besides, he had to make absolutely sure that his children. . . .

His children. She'd had to come to terms with the fact of their existence nine years before, those children whom she had agreed it would be wrong of him to leave, yes, even for her; and now it seemed she was to share them. Joy flooded her.

'I'll have them, Alec! Of course I will, darling!'

'Once the break's behind me, once I can freely get in touch again. . . .'

He was going to tell Jean. Had he any idea how much that mattered to her, that a term should be put to their deception? In a handful of words he'd made her a free woman, equal. And time would pass; it always did.

The night before he left they'd clung together, comforting each other for the chasm which lay between that and their next embrace. But time would pass, and then. . . .

So time had passed; and now the break was behind him. Or so the doorman had said. So much for time.

Why had she agreed not to write, not to phone? And had it been his idea or hers? She no longer remembered. But she'd agreed, yes; and she'd honoured her agreement even though that time which would pass, which was still on her side, dragged intolerably on. Because she was so sure of him.

Sure? Was she? Or was it that she'd invested so much in Alec Burroughs that she dared not be anything but sure? What about her pitiful inadequacy over Lorraine Hampstead, her fear of seeing the pair of them talking together in the lunch queue in case it wasn't mere chance? Just in case.

Oh, it had been insane, irrational, that sick and evil dread, that fantasy of loss! But hadn't this, too, been in her mind when she'd encouraged Alec to go North – that he wouldn't, in that new job, see Lorraine Hampstead every day?

All the same, his silence, that wasn't reasonable, either – my God, it wasn't reasonable!

'Well, is it?' she asked him. 'Do *you* call it reasonable?'

She held herself ready, waiting for the blade to strike; for, reasonable or not, that wasn't the true question and the true question could no longer be dodged. Since Alec had failed to communicate, the true question must be *for whom* this divorce. Was there another Lorraine in that town in the North from which so arctic a silence now emanated? Worse, was there another Eva, another Jean?

'Who is she?' She thrust back a strand of hair which had stuck to her tear-dried cheek. 'I think you'd better

102

tell me all about it, Mister Burroughs. . . .'

Who, who, who? The word pumped out like arterial blood as her hostility erupted. It was unguessed at, that hostility; vicious, scalding, destructive. Yes, but she'd force him to look at what he'd done; make him see it with her eyes, feel in his own person the death he'd inflicted, acknowledge the pain. . . . Not that she wanted him now – God, no! All she wanted was justice; that, and to murder him.

She stopped in front of the tallboy. Driftwood? Hadn't she, for him, become no more than driftwood at the mercy of the tide?

She snatched up the lump of oak and hurled it across the room.

The telephone crashed to the floor. They came apart, the handset and the stand, lay uncoupled.

Eva was suddenly still. Her anger had left her, the frenzy of hurt gone. She was out in the ordinary world once more, where the wind might rattle the curtains, where day would follow night. Across the room herself then, and on her knees. Dialling tone? Thank God! Oh, thank God she was still in touch!

She picked up the phone and replaced it on the table by her bed. She checked that the handset was truly in place. Because wasn't that what love was about, what prayer was about, being in touch?

She could stand back from it now, her rage; and she was appalled by that well of bitter water she'd glimpsed within. Love? This? Yet she did love him. So had love a dark, another face?

She returned the driftwood to the tallboy, but the bills which it had secured had scattered on the draught. She recalled how they'd risen like a flight of gulls about her head while she, intent on her own wild fancy, had glared through that reckoning of wings.

Absently, she pulled on her wrap, picked a silk square from the floor, its texture a nuance only. She stood for a while looking at it, that pattern which nothing could now change.

Patterns. She sat down on the edge of her bed, the scarf in her lap, considering patterns. Why had she been so quick to judge, so hasty to assume the worst? Was hers, then, a pattern of spite, not love? After all, what proof had she – to be vulgar, she told Pussy tiredly – that Alec had ditched her? Yet she'd reacted as though it were a certainty, she, who should have learnt that lesson once and for all over Lorraine Hampstead. Because fragmented, reassembled, those facts about Alec, what a very different pattern the same pieces made.

The curtains lifted, fell again. The wind came coldly in from the street and she fancied she could smell snow. Frost in May? It was always possible.

She shut the window and began to pace the room, urgent again but with an urgency for the truth not an urgency for vengeance; and, awed, she watched the pattern change, every scrap fitting, each piece snug. Whole as a rising bubble, as full of promise as the month of May, hope was given back to her.

She stood still, her hand to her cheek, ashamed. She was calm now, objective; and calmly, objectively, she surveyed and admitted her suspicion, jealousy, weakness, dread and all the manifold sins and wickednesses which she from time to time most grievously had committed – not necessarily because she wanted to commit them but because that's the way she was, Eva, and more the pity that it should be so. Yet Alec loved her. What a miracle that he could!

But to think that all this while she'd been raging at a mirage, lacerating herself for a shadow! For the truth, surely, was that Jean had refused to be accommodating, would not connive – and what a world of difference was there. She had given him his freedom, yes, but in her own time, on her own terms; and, torn, Eva guessed what those conditions might have been. Alec had, at last, told her the truth. Could she not have used that truth to fight him for their children?

Every piece fitted, was at home within the whole; yet

they were the same pieces, the ones which at first had so distressed her. She was amazed at her blindness.

Even his silence made sense now. How could he have written about a thing like that – the timing not his own, the shock of Jean and the children and, yes, for she knew her Alec, his vanity affronted? It must have been a cataclysm.

No, he hadn't written that letter she'd been waiting for but he had kept faith. Because one thing was certain: Alec hadn't come to Tigby for the opening of Salwart's Folly; assuming she'd be back, he'd come to Tigby to see her.

She picked up his bon voyage card. That idiot holiday! If only it had lasted for two weeks instead of three.

She began to move about the room, swift, neat-fingered, putting her affairs to rights. She recovered the bills from the floor, twinned and racked her shoes, separated dirty linen from clean. It was all clear to her now; she understood everything. The official opening would be his cover, an excuse for coming; for he'd need an excuse, Alec, even to himself, a mask for his pride, something to get him over the hump. For, the wreckage apart, he'd be feeling guilty about neglecting her; would be awkward, on the defensive, until he saw how she was taking it; might even – who knows? – be blaming her for what had happened. A last-minute decision, that's what he'd said to Peter. Well, it figured. The one thing he never would do was let her know his movements in advance.

She smiled as she considered that arrogant – yes, arrogant – assumption that she ought always to be available when it crossed his mind to need her – dear, awful Alec! But this time she hadn't been available.

Eva looked out on to the deserted street, which, in the lamplight, had an air of having been preserved in some chill and pallid jelly. Had they twitched, she wondered, those curtains in the house opposite when Alec walked up her path? Probably. Little passed unnoticed here.

She saw so clearly how it must have been. He'd have driven straight here, now that he'd nerved himself to come to Tigby, consumed with longing to tumble it all out – yes, and explain the awkward bits away, but no matter. The thing is he had come to see her, to tell her himself, to keep faith.

And then to find her still away.

How long had he stood in her porch before going off in his best suit and clean white shirt to witness the charade of the opening of the new building which they would never now share?

If only he'd left a note! But, no, that wasn't his way. Mrs Breem might read it; anybody might read it. Besides, Eva should have been here. Waiting. On the off-chance. Oh, Alec!

So what, indeed, was there left for him to do – he so inept in all but graphs and figures – but, under the umbrella of general bonhomie, enquiring about every woman whose name he could dredge up, ask also how Eva Wootton was these days, and leave with Peter Elliot a message which, though oblique, would signal her to contact him when she returned. What wouldn't cross his mind was that she might never get his message at all. As well she might not have done.

Thank God for drink, eh? she told Pussy.

Her room was nearly straight now. Just a couple more items in her suitcase, and then the case itself, to stow away. But should she ring or write? Her hands found the package as she pondered it. Nora's shawl.

She stood for a while holding it close, imagining Nora in it, regretting. And that letter – if only it could be waiting when she next looked in! At the same time the question throbbed on in her head: ring or write? Oil and water, the two emotions; and no way to make emotions emulsify.

13

In the end she settled for a letter, for what could she say when at last she heard his voice again but Alec, Alec, Alec like water flowing over a parched tongue?

More than that was needed. She had to be practical; and, to be practical, what if he'd let Jean keep the house? And to ring, unarmed, and get Jean – heavens, no! There was nothing for it but to write.

But it was going to be difficult, that letter, for it was important that she should get through to him at the right level; and Eva paused to reflect on the differing levels at which people lived. She, as she knew to her cost, was a deep-sea diver, but Alec seemed happier skating on the water's skin – neither better than the other but different, yes, and she must remember it; for though her nature might instruct her to lavish a welcome and spill out her longing it wouldn't do, not with this gentleman. From a firework display one good sparkler perhaps, from a vineyard a small glass of wine, from a flowering forest a single bloom – enough to make her point but never to terrify, to overwhelm.

The trouble was, though, that her nature would have none of her reason. Already composing themselves in her head, sentences took off like rockets, illuminating the darkness with glorious, prodigal fire and filling the air with grace.

So calculation lost to joy. The few lines she scribbled came out whole, complete, right: the only thing Eva Wootton could possibly have said, the only way, being herself, Eva could possibly have said it.

Within less than a minute she was asleep.

The door of number seven slammed as Eva turned out of her gate. Ollie Tucker passed her on the corner of Old Road.

'Nice day again.'

'Oh, isn't it! I. . . .'

She'd have been glad to walk in with Ollie Tucker; but, glancing at his watch, he hurried off intent, apparently, on getting to the station in exactly the same number of minutes as usual. It was surprising, really, that he'd noticed what the morning was like.

But, yes, it was a lovely morning. The horse chestnuts were beside themselves with beauty, their white candles, raised by spread and offering leaves, like incandescent praise. Eva grinned up at them like a child, like a clown, like a woman who has just written to her lover.

She had decided to post Alec's letter at the main sorting office. She was suddenly fearful for its safety, and which of all those red pillar boxes was without some latent hazard. Suppose the letter got wedged out of sight and was never found? Suppose the van driver let it drop before it reached his sack? Or went mad and stuffed it down a drain? Or some bored lout poured in petrol and set fire to it?

Don't be so bloody daft, she told Pussy.

All the same, she could do with a walk, a good long walk, like to the sorting office. After which she'd stay in town till the bus station opened; for on a morning like this, feeling like this, she could not believe that it hadn't been found, that mauve envelope with the stiff, distinctive writing. But when had Nora written it? Eva wondered suddenly. She hadn't noticed whether the ink was faded but had observed the vigour of the strokes.

At the end of Old Road, Eva turned left and descended through a grid of modest Victorian streets set about with panther-scabbed plane trees. Here, there were decent, hard-worked-for little houses which had known their station in life and seen no reason to be ashamed of it, even though it had been Yes, Ma'am, with a bob. And there was evidence of proper pride in those streets still, which was interesting. They were a damned sight cleaner than the town centre. No longer prim, though. At odds with the modesty of the slate roofs and iron railings, scarlet, vermilion, banana-yellow exploded on gateways and doors. And why not? In Tigby's mean winter when the townscape was so often no more than grey grudgingly conceived on grey she, too, longed for brightness; but to an eye unaccustomed to seasons how despairing the light of England must seem, and how comforting to simulate, if only on one's front door, the colours of home.

The people who complained of Railway Terrace, she'd noticed, never mentioned General Gordon Street or Scutari Lane where the doorsteps were far cleaner than the steps of the Town Hall. And Councillor Thornby, with his passion to keep Tigby white, hadn't it ever occurred to him that louts like Harry, the dairy trainee, were white? That loutishness and ugly living had nothing to do with colour but only with being a Stone Age person within?

The Johnsons! Heavens, she still hadn't seen them. Nor, for that matter, had she spoken to Bob, and it was important to do both.

All the same, Railway Terrace. . . . It was ugly, as any ghetto must be ugly; and it did make her uneasy – it shouldn't perhaps, but it did – when she found herself there, the only white face. Was it because she felt she symbolised a hostility she didn't feel? Or was it that everything had happened too fast, that it took more than the lifetime one was allowed to flush out those unreasoning terrors from the untaught heart? And, remembering Thornby again, I'm glad, Eva thought, defiant, that he died when he did; that he never had a chance to look at Railway Terrace as it is now and turn round and say I told you so. Because he'd still have been wrong, but how could I have proved it to him?

Eva circumvented the park which, at this hour, was still locked, bolted and barred like the wretched couple she lived opposite, and found herself in The Avenue. This was another world, a spacious world which Scutari Lane and General Gordon Street had sprung into being to serve. But that time had passed; and now those detached stone mansions with their ponderous porches and fantasies of turret and gable end, their Scots pines moulting, had been dragged into a today of rented rooms and flatlets. Dirty milk-bottles and dustbins spilled out on to the pavement while the house beyond kept themselves to themselves like distressed gentlewomen fallen on hard times.

She was distracted by sparrows twittering over a half-eaten sandwich as, belly low, eye intent, a cat moved in, smooth as black oil.

'Shoo! Giddorf!' Eva said; but half-heartedly, for a cat must hunt. To make amends she stroked it; and the cat followed her east as far as the canal bridge.

And once over the canal bridge and past the railway station there was the sorting office.

Eva stood for a minute looking down at the envelope, at her own neat writing which – oh, but precisely when? – would alert Alec at his office desk. Marked *personal*, of course, and Alec addressed formally by rank – a fact which suddenly took her aback. It was as though she'd inadvertently accosted a strange man. Then she blinked light-headedly at the heavy brass-framed slot. Her letter was on its way.

She'd written to Alec at last, and the letter was on its way!

But what now was she to do with all this exhilaration, this tyrannical exhilaration? How could she channel it? She felt she'd never be tired again. Tired? What, with her letter on its way and her heart like a singing bird whose nest is in a. In a. Was it watered shoot or waterspout? she asked Pussy.

A little mottled dog with spring in his paws but no tail to speak of, no more to speak of than the butt of a cigar, trotted across the road. Never mind, Eva told him. What does a tail matter if a dog has style?

She felt at one with that springy little dog – and why not, with life pounding through her and her heart like whatever it was the Rossetti woman had been on about? No longer the dispirited old lady who'd hobbled from the crematorium but a goddess ten feet tall and girt for victory, Eva swung off down the street which led to the town centre.

It was a gilded, glinting morning full of sharp lines, brilliant planes, dark blue depths. If she'd been a painter, who would it most satisfy her to have been? El Greco? Storm skies with caverns of luminosity. A drama of harvested light which charged with shadow all but the agony of the crucified. Or Cotman, truthful and quiet, who could paint as if through rain?

Well, she'd never be anyone significant now – how could she be, at sixty? – but there had been a time when Nora, poor Nora, had thought she had something in her – and not Nora alone. So there it was. They were wrong. She was just Eva Wootton – though, at the moment, not too displeased to be Eva, tally-ho!

Oh, but the smells! Mossy, a bit rank, alongside the canal where a scarf of mist hung like a levitating ghost; sweet and damp near the bushes; acrid by the wood-yard – how important they were, smells. She sniffed at her palms. Faintly herbal – rosemary? thyme? – and a suggestion of Marie biscuit. Her senses, skinned by joy, leapt to welcome each novelty. Life, life – yes, please! Lots of it! More!

Something, though, was niggling. For heaven's sake, of course! She was hungry! When had she last eaten? She couldn't remember – and imagine it, Pussy, not knowing a thing like that!

A panegyric to food burst into song in her head – bacon, eggs, toast. . . . And pints of scalding tea, hey nonny nonny! Joe's – that was the answer;

Joe's in the covered market. It would be open by now. And, Pussy, how she'd eat! Who, given the chance, wouldn't elect to be Eva Wootton, now in the sixty-first year of her youth? Yes, and about to have breakfast.

Hot-foot for Joe's, she nevertheless paused at the Concourse where Tigby's one stick of bombs had fallen during the war, razing a Georgian square – Francini ceilings, sedan chair hoists, link-extinguishers, the lot; she'd seen the photographs. It was now a pedestrian precinct, the proud achievement of the mob – thank you, Peter, Bert – elected the time before the time before the last, and Eva lingered to deplore it. Pink and ochre paving stones were set out like slices of some mind-blowing Battenburg cake with invalid prunus wilting in regulated gaps between. A chorus line of stores, tarty and strident, elbowed for attention, competing with a huddle of boutiques, up-market, for the better class of customer. And everywhere strip lighting, some still, some in flux, come-hither, like awful eyelids; and litter everywhere too, graffiti everywhere on those concrete, impermanent walls. Everywhere altars to the flimsy, the cheap, the throw-away. No sense of history, no revulsion from ugliness, no energy but to acquire or deface.

Eva surveyed the walls. Who were they, these ubiquitous malcontents? They weren't all illiterate. Some could spell words as difficult as democracy and government yet seemed to have nothing but contempt for law and no conception of order. There was a new slogan today – *FUCK THE TORY'S* – sprayed in letters two feet high, and she was ashamed to note that the error comforted her. Perhaps it was her age – no doubt it was – but she found loutishness easier to forgive if she could equate it with educational deprivation.

ANARCH . . ., she read, scowling; then grinned with delight. On to the truncated protest a quieter hand had added, *angel?*

Then, suddenly, she was drenched with longing to be

there, at Joe's; and not just to sit and eat, though that would be fine, but to peg herself to the ordinary world again by the simple act of sitting down in a public place and ordering food. For the drama was over. Those anguished, arid months were a thing of the past. What she needed now was for life to keep still, to stay ordinary, so that within the framework of that unexciting ordinariness she could accommodate to the fact that she'd written to Alec at last, that Alec would now ring.

14

As Eva put her hand to the door it opened and a man stepped out. In spite of the promise of the morning he wore a khaki muffler and a long drab coat with a lovat tweed cap.

Eva stepped aside to let him pass, aware of a faint smell of sweat and chips. She glanced up questioningly when he didn't.

'Excuse me. . . .'

Polite but firm. Nice lady, really; just wanting like hell to get inside and sit down.

The cap, whipped off now, was clamped against his chest, the splayed hand pink as a giant starfish. Cheeks blushing; childish eyes, blankly blue, frankly admiring – he *fancied* her, the starfish man? Good God!

'It's me, Mrs Wootton. Bob. The milkman.'

'Oh, *Bob* . . .!'

'Didn't know me, did you? I'd know you, Mrs Wootton; I'd know you anywhere, that's the truth. I'd know you all right.'

'It's just that I wasn't expecting. . . . But you haven't left the dairy, have you, Bob?'

'It's my day off, Wednesday – you forgotten, 'aven't you? Nah, it's never me brings your milk Wednesdays. I never brought your milk once, not on a Wednesday. Wednesday's my—'

'Well, enjoy your day off,' she said briskly, trying to get past.

'Here, when you coming to see my trains, Mrs Wootton?'

'Trains?'

114

'My 'obby. I told you. Don't say you forgot that, too,'
he said indulgently, 'that I got an 'obby. Still, we all
make mistakes, eh? Live and . . .'

'I'd love to,' she lied, 'one of these days. . . .'

He nailed her.

'Sunday, then.'

'Well. . . .'

'I asked my old lady if I could 'ave you to tea some
Sunday and she said yes. See you Sunday, then. It's a
good day, Sunday. We cuts the cake Sundays. Always
'ave. So long as I can remember,' Bob said with an air of
revelation, 'we've cut the cake Sundays. Never
varies. . . .'

Mnya! Her mouth seemed to be stuffed with cotton
waste. She said with sudden decisiveness: 'Look, Bob,
I'm afraid I really must go.'

'You'll come to tea, though, Sunday. It's. . . .'

The market was burgeoning around her. She watched
a man and woman furnishing their stall – approach-
ing, retreating, lifting, building. Under their hands
grew pyramids of oranges, of lemons, of glossy,
polyurethaned apples. There were cauliflowers, too,
each one perfect, a bride's pale posy sheathed in green.
Bride missing, however. Not ancient mariner, though,
my God! Eva stifled a yawn. The wedding guest sat on
a stone, she pointed out to Pussy. Lucky old wedding
guest!

'. . . Number nineteen Albert Terrace,' Bob was saying. 'Y'know Albert Terrace? Yeah, well, we live at
nineteen. There's a pub, the White 'Art, and number
nineteen's opposite. It sort of bulges on the corner and
you can't miss it because there's a pub. . . .'

'The White Hart,' Eva put in quickly.

'You got it all right this time, 'aven't you?' Bob
congratulated her. 'See you Sunday, Mrs Wootton.
Teatime.'

He was about to go. She remembered then, hesitated.
But, no, she must.

'Bob. . . .'

'Yeah?' he said, turning back.

'About Harry. . . .'

''Arry?'

'Yes, I want a word with you about. . . .'

''Arry? 'Arry's my assistant. I'm learning 'im. You seen him, Mrs Wootton; 'e's on the round. . . .'

'I've seen him all right! Did you know that last Monday morning . . .?'

''Ere, did I tell you 'Arry could've gone to college? 'E won it,' Bob explained. 'It was 'is right, only he didn't see no point . . .'

'Bob!'

'That's what killed 'is dad, y'know. Or so they reckon. 'Arry not going to college. Set 'is 'eart on it, 'is dad 'ad. . . .'

So he had a father, a family, had he, this specimen lout? Lived in a home without a capital aitch. Wasn't deprived, then, as she, Eva, was deprived who hadn't a clue who her daddy was nor her mummy neither. Hadn't that excuse – hadn't, damn it, any excuse . . .!

She found herself shouting. The couple at the stall opposite glanced up, looked away.

'Harry pulled up the Johnsons' tulips – deliberately destroyed them! Threw them on the grass!'

'Wha'?'

'You heard what I said. That bastard Harry stopped behind when you'd gone and . . .'

''Arry? 'Arry ain't no bastard,' Bob said indignantly. 'Y'didn't oughter say things like that, Mrs Wootton, like 'Arry's a bastard when 'e ain't. Nah, 'Arry's Councillor Thornby's boy; 'e ain't no bastard. Councillor Thornby as was, I should say, because 'Arry killed 'im; leastwise that's what. . . .'

Eva leant against the wall of Joe's and held on to the window-ledge. Without warning, the market had begun to move as on a slowly revolving drum, everything in stately flux about her. Ill? She couldn't be. Just hungry. Don't look for a minute, she advised herself.

From the void the voice went on: '. . .' Arry Thornby.

That's 'is name, and legal, too. Ever so kind 'e was, 'is dad. Stood up to the Welfare for my old lady and got 'er 'er supplementary. We all voted for 'im in our street, Councillor Thornby. When 'e was alive, of course. A real gent. Pity as 'Arry killed 'im but, then, if 'e didn't see no point. . . .'

God, how she hated Tigby! Alec apart, how marvellous it would be to get away from these mean, tweaked curtains, corseted obscenities, the boredom. To stop feeling that one's head was forever trapped in a paper bag. To give the spirit room to breathe. She wanted life to be ordinary but she didn't mean this.

Silence. Her giddiness had gone, the nausea was going. Cautiously, Eva opened her eyes. Bob, gaping into the distance, was picking his nose. He turned when she moved, replaced his cap.

''Ere, I better get on. I got the shopping to do for my old lady. See you Sunday, then.'

'Number nineteen Albert Terrace,' Eva said, limp. 'Teatime.'

But where had all that exhilaration gone? Where was the goddess now, how long ago youth?

'*So look who's here!*' carolled a voice behind her as she pushed at the door. Doris Cope. Eva waited for it. 'Ships that pass in the night! You bring out the poet in me – always did. Well, how are you, stranger?'

'Fine, fine!' Eva cried, baring her teeth. 'Lovely to see you,' she managed to say. 'Oh, and thanks for your letter.'

'So which classes are you . . .?'

'I've only just got back, for God's sake!' Eva said irritably. 'Give me a chance to wash my smalls. Anyway, I'm about to have breakfast.'

'If you got back on Monday you should have washed your smalls by this.' Doris followed her in. 'I'll have a cup with you, since you seem to be set on it, though it's a rip-off, having it out.'

'I was up early.'

'So was I up early. I like to do my marketing early,

117

like the French. You're not the only one with continental habits, you know.' Smartly dressed, on the scraggy side of lean, Doris scrutinised Eva from her six feet one. 'Well, I've seen you looking bonnier, I must say. Burning the candle at both ends, I suppose. All those chaps, was it?' she asked hungrily. 'Got a nice tan, though. Lovely. Or is it out of a bottle? Oh,' she said, remembering, 'I was *so* sorry to see your old friend had passed away. It was after I'd written or I'd have said something. Still, I expect it was a mercy. I certainly don't want to hang on; not when my time comes, I mean. There's a lot in euthanasia only, as usual, the Chruch stands in the way of progress. So what was it like, that holiday of yours?'

What was it like, that holiday of hers? 'Fine,' she said again, and was saved from more by the necessity of ordering.

'You're never going to eat bacon *and* egg!' Doris exclaimed.

'Why not?'

'What about all the calories?'

'What about them? I'm hungry.'

It was no longer true. The sight of the fatty bacon and glaucous egg sickened her. But it was an excuse to sit on; and she drank cup after cup of tea as she pushed the food about her plate and prayed for Doris Cope to go.

'No, you definitely ought to do something with your hands,' Doris was saying for the third time. 'I'm not being critical, and yoga's all very well, I'm sure, but don't tell me it'll stop you moping. Now, macramé. . . .'

Moping? Do I mope, Pussy? 'I don't mope,' Eva said, wondering whether the greyness where all of Eva now lurked save this bright and outward face was what Doris meant by moping.

'Then you could fool me.' Doris looked at her, dissatisfied. 'You can't tell me a thing about your holiday, for instance. All that money and nothing to show for it but a yellow skin. Well, there you are; I bet it's because you were moping. Now something like macramé, something to get your teeth into, that'd really take you out of yourself. . . .'She veiled her eyes. 'How's your friend, by the way?'

'Which friend?'

'*Which* friend! There you go again! I've never known anyone so secretive in my . . .'

'Oh, Alec? Fine.' Eva listened as alien words came out of her. 'A little thicker-set, or so I hear; and doing very nicely in his new job. He was in Tigby last week. . . .'

Doris pounced.

'So he didn't realise you'd gone abroad! Why hadn't you told him?'

'Of course he knew. He sent me a bon voyage card; but, as usual, he muddled the dates – you know what men are – and . . .'

'*I* know what men are . . .!' Where had she heard that recently? '. . . Sods, the lot of them – pardon my French. I've had my adventures, too, you know; only, *I* kept my head,' Doris said, tossing it. 'Well, so he's been at last, has he? When are you joining him, then?'

Eva clenched her hands under the table as she tried to smile.

'Really, Doris! There are some questions. . . .'

'Oh, all right, all right; I can take a hint as well as the next. . . . Mind your own business, I always say, and let others mind theirs. Anyway, I'm glad for your sake he's been. When are you putting your house on the market?'

Eva was startled out of her misery. Putting her house on the market? All these practicalities! She'd have to in the end, of course, but. . . .

'Oh, time enough for that when. . . .'

'When?'

Bloody Doris Cope! And always boasting of her tact!

'When it suits me,' she said, bland.

'What I'm getting at – I mean if you do get round to

119

thinking of it seriously – is I could be interested in it myself. It's nice and fresh out your way, isn't it? Almost country. I've always fancied Barnes Farm Close as a neighbourhood. . . . And we could save on the deal; no agents' fees. . . .'

'But what about my neighbours, Doris?' Eva asked maliciously. 'Had you forgotten the West Indian family next door?'

'What, the Johnsons? Oh, but haven't you . . .?' Doris pulled herself up. She gave Eva a curious look. 'I thought you said they were very nice,' she amended.

'And so they are. They're dear friends; I just don't see enough of them these days, unfortunately. But with your views about. . . .'

'Well, they won't be there for ever; and with house prices soaring. . . . If you and I could agree a price between us, we'd be laughing, really, dealing direct . . . .'

Eva looked at her watch.

'Of course.'

'So you'll bear it in mind if . . .?'

'I'll bear it in mind.'

Doris fidgeted.

'Where are you going after this?'

'To the bus office. I dropped a letter and . . .'

'A letter? You mean from this Alec man?'

Had it been in her hand Doris would have gone to almost any lengths just to glimpse the writing.

'A letter,' Eva said equably. 'I want to collect it, that's all.'

Odd how one could live on two levels at the same time.

'Are you ready to go, then?'

'No.'

'Oh, well, all right; I'd better say ta-ta. I can't hang around all morning,' Doris said, getting up. She gave Eva's plate a distasteful glance. 'Do stop messing that about, Eva! Either eat it or leave it alone. And don't forget what I said about macramé – and mind you sign up early; it's always oversubscribed. Anyway, I'll pop in on you before that to see what you've decided about the house. You're sure to be around now you're a lady of leisure. . . .'

She had a drab image of roots winkling greyly down from her elbows and anchoring her to the table-top. Impossible to move. Impossible.

Not her table, though; Joe's. She examined it for the first time, now she was alone, that table where she might take root. Plastic. Falsely marble. Like cheap corned beef striated with fat; green corned beef, putrescent. On it, between her elbows, an empty cup with a saucer; Joe's, too.

Doris, thank God, had gone. But so had her lightness of mood. Exhilaration? That belonged to another Eva, a different age. Now was lead and clay, and she an ageing woman who'd sat up all night writing to her lover – or so it seemed – instead of going sensibly to bed, early, with a glass of hot milk and honey.

Which brought her back to the letter, to both letters: Nora's, which might never be found, and Alec's. . . .

Eva shut her eyes. But it was a good letter, she protested wearily as she tried not to recall the specific words which had made it so.

Joe's table again, those striations. And what a dilemma it was, this uneasy juxtapositioning of flesh and spirit! For who could separate that marbled grain, set need against resource and sit in judgement on the children of necessity? Not she.

She was alerted in spite of the mud, the lead, in spite of the dreary and now dominant self. For who could separate that marbled grain . . .? Iambic pentameter. William hadn't written it, she could swear to that; so who . . .?

'Fool!' she said under her breath, just enough aware to glance around, make sure she hadn't been observed.

For nobody had written it. The table-top had written it. All right, then, *she* had written it.

'Contain yourself, Student! Prithee no more poesy!'

In spite of herself and all that dominant mud, she grinned. Dear Idris! *Contain yourself, Student . . .*!

Splendid advice, she told Pussy. We ought to try following it some time.

But he hadn't contained himself, had he, Dr Idris Lloyd, when he'd heard that she'd turned down the award?

Better not think of that, though, she warned Pussy; we've troubles enough as it is.

Which, again, brought her back to her letter to Alec. The letter she'd sent off as if on wings. That letter which was now on its way. It was a good letter, yes, a very good letter; she knew that. There was nothing wrong with the letter except, perhaps, one thing – no, two. Was this the letter Alec would want to receive? Should she have written at all?

It was no on both counts.

Mechanically, she glanced at her watch. Nausea swilled in her diaphragm transmitting signals of unease; and, God, she was tired. She rested her head on her hands – just for the minute only, sweetheart.

Eva jerked violently, saved herself from the abyss, was confused to find herself in Joe's. She remembered then and, her heart still thumping from the dread of that inner cliff-fall, looked again at her watch. Four minutes had passed, only four; but during that sliver of time it seemed that she had been on a momentous journey. There was a landscape she'd recognised, and something she both knew and didn't know – what?

She blinked sore eyes and looked into herself. The landscape was marbling away as, protean, the actors changed role; and from all that panorama which had stretched out before her she snatched back no more than a tiny twig from the tree of knowledge. She had gone to the Shaven Crown and found no one at reception.

How stupid can I get? she fretted.

But the sense of rejection stayed. It lay like a stone,

reinforcing the certainty which had already crystallised in her. No, she should not have given way to joy; caution should have prevailed. She ought to have waited for Alec to contact her. The letter was a mistake.

A couple of hours ago she'd been exhilarated, confident; now her cheeks burnt with shame. Yet the facts hadn't changed. Nothing had changed except her inner climate, that black hole which had opened in herself, swallowed her up. Did that change facts?

Apparently it did. Facts? What fact was there now apart from that black hole? How could there be other facts when she was inside it?

After a while she whispered: 'Alec. . . .'

She listened as the word dropped into the air. She imagined ripples spreading from it to widen into glassy rings which slapped against the containing walls, troubling invisible rushes at the air's brink and causing ducks to bob, buoyant and upheld, on the skin of the ensuing silence.

(Prithee no more poesy.)

Shelled in that silence, Eva imagined a telephone. She stared at it until the image began to pulse on her vision.

15

'So where were you off to, my dear, so early this morning?'

Marty Pike in a dark suit, very sharp, laid back. And a new briefcase, too. Eva noticed it in spite of herself: real leather with a gold monogram.

He was already on his way out; but he turned back, putting that new briefcase carefully aside. And what can I get you, my dear? A favour. He told her so; that he didn't serve in the shop now, not normally: he hadn't the time. He was too busy these days – looking at her hard – with more important things.

She didn't take the bait.

Apples? Of course. He paused, giving Eva time to squint at the scales; then, ostentatiously wiping it, he took up another apple, the largest and best of the lot, and added it to the pan.

'How do you know I was out early?'

'*The eyes, ears, voice and conscience of Tigby* – didn't you read my manifesto? Which reminds me: I'm still waiting for a certain lady to congratulate a certain councillor. . . .'

'Oh. Congratulations, Councillor . . .' He detected the grudging note and smirked. 'Actually, I didn't hear till. . . . You've given me too many apples,' she said sharply. 'I asked for a pound, not a pound and a half!'

'And I'm only charging you for a pound.' Smooth as silk. 'The extra apple is a tribute. For Eve, from the old Adam.'

'In the days when I went to church,' she snapped, 'it

was Eve gave Adam the apple. And there was a snake involved, I seem to recall.'

'There!' he admired, eyes glinting. 'Wit, wisdom and learning as well as comeliness and womanly charm! And when', he asked in an undertone, following her to the door, 'are you going to let me take you for a drive?'

'It was the gravel pits last time you tried it on, Councillor Pike.'

'A drive to the gravel pits, then. Which are – or so I'm informed by the *cognoscenti* – an ecologists' paradise.'

'Those are long words, Councillor.'

Oh, Marty was on form all right. And success had plumped him out. She noted it from worlds away, those grey worlds where instinct betrayed one and lost letters were not found.

'It must', he was saying, 'be all the committees I serve on. Or' (serenely) 'chair. You've no idea of the words some of them use. It's opened my eyes, anyway. Yes, it's being quite an education; and, after all, committees', he pronounced, 'are the lifeblood of democracy, and democracy's what I'm in business about.'

'Lifeblood?' she queried, malicious. 'I thought you said bows and arrows, Councillor Pike.'

'*Swords and bucklers*, my dear, to quote. However, as I soon discovered, the ill-informed don't know what bucklers are; whereas lifeblood. . . .' He repeated it with some satisfaction: 'The lifeblood of democracy. It sounds well,' he told her.

'Oh, yes? And what about the death pangs of democracy?' She couldn't help herself; she snarled: 'Corporate management, for example?'

Nothing to do with her any more. Didn't care anyway – why should she? But just saying it made her angry. She glared at him, almost spat them out, those words.

Marty Pike beamed fondly back.

'Rule number one: keep cool in debate. And you shouldn't dismiss corporate management so lightly, you really should not. It's a prized weapon in the armoury of democratic procedure. It ties up officers in meetings about things which don't concern them and they get so worn out reading mountains of paper about topics they've no interest in that the members elected by the will of the people can carry out that will in whatever way they think fit without too much interference from professional crackpots who seem to imagine money grows on trees. That's democratic enough, surely?'

'You're being very frank!' Eva snorted.

'Why not?' Significant pause. 'Between friends.' She didn't take him up. 'No,' he went on, 'it was a wonderful thing for democracy, the reorganisation of local government back in 1974. For one thing, it did away with all that pie-in-the-sky stuff. It put priorities into perspective. It got us back to basics. Money.'

Why didn't she slap his face and go? Or, come to that, just go? But she stood on, struggling to get her own priorities into perspective, get back to her own basics. Meanwhile, time must be helped to pass and preferably not alone.

'Take, for example,' Marty was saying, 'that great spender, education. For nearly a hundred years it could act more or less independent of the political arm, but not any more. We politicians take those educational decisions now, and we take them for party political reasons. And', he said with satisfaction, 'I for one glory in it.'

'Yes,' Eva said, 'I dare say you do.'

'Come, now, my dear, think a moment. You're a ratepayer yourself. Don't tell me you want your rates rocketing just to pay for them frills – those frills – which aren't a blind bit of use to anyone, least of all the kiddies.'

'I was thinking about the efficient running of the service.'

'And I', he said, watching her, 'was thinking about the maypoles. Five thousand pounds it was going to cost for kiddies to dance in their frilly knickers. . . . You did hear, of course, about the maypoles?'

'Yes; but never mind about the maypoles. I also heard – I know from first hand – what's happened to the secretaries.'

'Ah, the secretaries! Yes. You'd have a special interest in the ancillary services, my dear, wouldn't you?'

'Yes, I would, if that's what you're calling secretaries these days.'

'And only natural,' he reassured her. 'But time marches on; and one mustn't allow personal feelings to impede the passage of progress, must we?'

'Progress? You call it progress, putting skilled secretaries into a typing pool?'

'Progress depends', he told her, 'on the assessing and redeploying of our resources for maximum exploitation within the limits of the budget available at a time of planned non-growth.'

Eva found that he'd taken hold of her elbow. She looked at him fiercely, but Marty Pike smiled back, benign. Couldn't tweak it away, though, that elbow, without making a scene. He had quite a grip, as she recalled. Anyway, why bother? She was in a relatively public place.

She allowed him to lead her down the passage which divided his shop from the next.

'Well, Councillor, what's all this in aid of?'

They stood in his back yard facing each other. Surprisingly neat, that yard, she noticed. Tidily-stacked boxes, fruit trays; a row of clean bins exactly aligned side by side. His truck – *M. J. R. PIKE: SERVING TO HELP YOU, HELPING TO SERVE YOU* – had been so recently washed down that it was still wet. The concrete, too, had been brushed and swilled. From the back of her mind she approved it all. There wasn't so much as a straw that shouldn't be there.

But there was no one else there, either. Eva noted that, too, and tensed her muscles. Even though she felt dreadful and everything was too much effort. Even though she felt she'd left herself nothing to live for, that her life might be as good as over, thanks to that idiot letter. Even so, she tensed her muscles, was on the defensive, prepared to fight – funny, that.

'So?' she asked him, watchful.

'I've a business proposition to put to you, Miss Wootton.'

Formal. Very correct. (*Very* correct? OK, correct. Dear old Idris Lloyd.)

'A business proposition, Councillor Pike?'

'May I call you Eva?'

'No.'

He laughed, came closer.

'What a woman, eh? You know, I *like* your spirit, my dear. . . .'

'I thought', she pointed out, 'that you had a business. . . .'

His face was suddenly hard. It took her aback, that straight look.

'And so I have. Do you want a job?' He measured her. 'A good job?'

Did she want a job – *did* she! Peter Elliot had said. . . . But it hadn't meant anything till now, till Marty Pike put it into words, that what she, Eva, needed was, above all, a job. For time must be got through, must be allowed to pass, till Alec . . . if Alec. . . . And how better to fill that time than with a job, good or not? Macramé she could laugh at.

'A job?' she asked; wary, though.

'That's what I said.'

She looked him over carefully. White slave traffic, Pussy? she hazarded. The thought almost lifted her spirits.

'And what kind of job would that be, Councillor Pike?'

'Secretarial,' he replied, unsmiling. 'In the new County Hall. On a higher grade than your last, and starting at a higher salary.'

Eva stared at him. County Hall? And on a higher grade than. . . .

'You mean . . .?'

'You could start Monday,' he said, still unsmiling.

She frowned in disbelief.

'But I've already turned down the pool, thank you very much! It's because I wouldn't work in the pool that—'

'I never said the pool. I said a secretarial job and I mean a secretarial job.' He eyed her coldly. It matters to him; it really matters. So watch it, she told herself. 'It's a key post and it's yours if you want it.'

'What post?' she asked, incredulous. Was there one? And if there was. . . .

'I asked if you wanted it.'

She tried to make her laugh light-hearted.

'I'm sixty, for God's sake; and that makes one hell of a difference! At sixty—'

'Not this time.' There was a pause. 'I've told you; if you want the job, you can have it.' Another pause. 'Do you want it?'

She began to protest: 'But I know nothing about it. . . . I mightn't be suitable. . . . It hasn't been advertised. . . . I haven't even been interviewed. . . .'

'You are suitable. There's no need for an advertisement. This is an interview and I'm offering you the job. Yes or no is all you need to say.'

She saw now why he'd got on. Not only did he relish power, he had an instinct for it and – how misled she'd been – natural authority which she hadn't even guessed at till now. *The Prince*, Tigby version. Marty Pike a backyard Machiavelli – good God!

'Well?' A faint smile. 'Eva?'

She flushed angrily.

'I said. . . .'

He smiled again, cold and composed.

'I'd think very, very, *very* carefully if I was you, my dear, before I turned down an offer like that,' he said softly. 'You could be the queen bee of the whole hive. . . .'

'Two verys too many!' she snapped. 'One would have

129

made your point.' (Bless you, Idris Lloyd.) She bit back a comment on the subjunctive, though. Don't kick a man in the balls when he hasn't any, she told Pussy.

But how *dare* he call her Eva when. . . .

Still, she felt better. Flaming bloody mad enough to feel better, even if just for the minute only, sweetheart.

'That tongue of yours,' he mourned, yearning at her, 'that tongue . . .!'

'What about my tongue?' she asked, tart.

'It's got you into trouble already, my dear; and it's going to get you into a lot more trouble if you don't learn to curb it. . . .' He was sorry for her, solicitous. 'You're altogether too impulsive. You need someone to take care of you. . . .'

His arm crept round her waist. But this time she was ready for him; and *wham*! she went on his instep, all her pent-up misery and rage smiting him through the heel of her shoe.

And it hurt like hell. She could see that.

When he could at last speak he said:'You don't know who your real friends are, do you? All the same, I like a girl with spirit and . . .'

'And I haven't yet learnt the price I'm to pay for this favour, have I?' she countered.

He looked at her in silence. Wrong. She did know the price she was to pay for that favour. She might have guessed. She said contemptuously: 'You can keep your job, then, Marty Pike. Find yourself another queen bee.'

His eyes were cold, but he was still patient.

'I said I'd think very carefully. . . .'

'Yes, I know. I heard you the first time. But there's nothing to think about. You can stuff your job, Councillor.'

A glint in his eyes. Not nice, but still quietish.

'Sleep on it all the same,' he advised. 'Sleep on it, my dear. You can let me have your answer tomorrow.' He looked at her, held her eye. 'And I wouldn't be too hasty, not if I was you.'

130

This time it burst from her before she could stop it: 'If I *were* you! Subjunctive.'

Waspish, like Gwen; school-ma'amy. She was appalled at her cheap little victory. And she hadn't intended to say it; not at all. Perhaps – revelation – that's what he'd meant about her tongue?

Eva squinted at Marty Pike. Oh dear. He's sick to the hairt, she told Pussy, and fain would lee doon.

She was still searching for what Marty would have called a formula, meaning a way of putting things right without losing face, when Marty spoke. He was still quiet – quiet now to the point of deadly. He'd come a long way in a short time, had Marty Pike – either that, or she'd underestimated him from the start.

'Well, then, that's it, Miss Wootton. . . .' Formal. *My dear* past history. No more free apples, cheap grapes. 'I'm sorry we can't see eye to eye, and I think you'll live to feel the same. To be frank, I'd have found your help very useful. With things', he said savagely, 'like the subjunctive, for instance. And I could have helped you; make no mistake about that. Oh, yes. There have been others', he said carefully, 'who weren't too proud to accept favours from. . . .' She watched him hesitate fractionally between *them* and *those*. '. . . People', he went on smoothly, 'in a position to lend a helping hand. Like – shall we say – my dear old friend Jack Thornby, a man sorely missed in this community. And I myself. . . .' Watching her. Choosing his words with care; words of an anti-personnel nature. '. . . I, too, had hoped to have had the privilege of putting something in your way as dear old Jack did last year for that chum of yours – what was his name? Burroughs? Yes, Alec Burroughs. . . .'

Was it from her, that sound? It was ripped out of someone.

'*What did you say?*'

'I think you heard,' Marty Pike said, smiling bleakly.

16

Eva let herself in, Marty's apples in her hand. The morning's mail was still on the mat and she picked it up. An offer of cheap life insurance for the elderly. Five pee off tinned peas. Win a Dream Home.

So that's why Alec had been so confident about getting his promotion. Jack Thornby had wangled the job.

The knowledge feasted on her like some obscene foetus, a lurching inner presence like that other foetus, her despair, with which it had twinned. Why hadn't she waited for Alec to act in his own good time? Why had he never told her about Jack Thornby?

And to think she'd imagined she'd charted the hazards in herself, achieved a dented peace! Would she never learn?

She stood on in the hall.

'Well?' she said fretfully. 'Well?'

Why didn't she sit down and read a book? When had she last read anything which could decently be called a book? Yet there had been a time when she'd devoured books; and she owned thousands of them. There were books all over the house, most of which she'd actually read. But not for a while. Not for a long while now. Which was another thing she wouldn't think about, just how long that while, and why.

And, no, she would not cry, she would not be sorry for herself, she would not repine. What was done was done; and if, in the house, she could find no escape from this imprisoning obsession which was Alec, well, then, she must go out again – out yet again; must walk her body forth into the sunlight and try to lose herself among her milling kind.

So out Eva went yet again, head high, chin up, a smile which felt like dried egg white on her face. And she made a point of stepping jauntily so that they would never guess – whoever they were, those people out there beyond her place of captivity – that this was a woman held to ransom by herself; that she was no more than a piece of flotsam, a lump of driftwood at the mercy of the tide.

Ed Johnson was at his gate examining the latch.

'Ed!' she cried. 'Oh, how *lovely* . . .!'

Her voice? Yes. What, that joyous one? Yes. Astonishing! How, though, was she going to explain Harry? And how those months of neglect?

'. . . I was just this minute coming round to say hello to Miriam!' she lied.

She skipped over the skimpy hedge which separated their front gardens. Ain't I volatile? A tired aside to Pussy. She brandished her handbag, too – good God – as though that frenetic gesture might make him believe her the more readily. Overdoing it as usual; yet wasn't that just what people expected of her, what they took reassurance from, that she should overdo it?

'. . . And where have you all *been*?'

Guilt showing now like the hem of her petticoat, for it was she who'd *been*, not they.

Edward Johnson straightened up. He stood for a further moment, hand on gate, then turned. She was shocked out of her act.

'Ed, love! Have you been ill?'

Impulsively, her hand went out to caress his arm. She felt him resist her and dropped her hand. Oh, no, not that stupid Ella Fitzgerald bit! He couldn't, surely he couldn't. . . .

'Good afternoon. . . .' He hesitated. '. . . Eva. You look well,' he told her. 'You've been on holiday?'

Polite, unsmiling, like the dead who can contain their

133

feelings. His eyes sought his own house, returned and found her still there. She began to chatter then, wanting the trouble, whatever it was, to go away; trying to put clocks back, make things be as they'd been before.

'... What with Alec going North, and all those ghastly changes at work – but that's a long story – and my deciding – oh, on the spur of the moment, you know – to retire, and ... and, of course. ...' She heard it come mindlessly out and blushed deeply. '... And, of course, Pussy dying. ...'

Pussy dying? Dear God! Edward Johnson inclined his head, made no comment. Eva floundered on.

'... What I mean, Ed, is I just don't know where time's gone. ... Anyway, I was just popping in' – popping in? – 'to see Miriam. Actually, I'd have been round this morning, only. ...'

'You're very kind, but my wife's not at home.' Ed glanced again at his windows. 'She's away for the day.'

'Oh,' Eva said, deflated. 'What time will she . . .?'

'Not till very late.'

She'd never known him to be brusque and edgy before. He opened his gate and stood aside to let her go.

'I tell you what,' she cried, an inspiration, 'why don't you both come in for a drink and a hunk of bread and something when Miriam gets back? I don't care how late. ...'

'It's very nice of you,' he said, hesitant. 'I appreciate. ...'

She clinched it: 'See you later, then.'

'No.'

'No?' she said, disappointed. 'Why, isn't she coming . . .?'

The door behind her crashed open hitting something with great violence. Startled, Eva swung round. Miriam Johnson was on the step.

'*Mirri!* But Ed thought you were. . . .'

The words were out before she could stop them, though she'd seen the hostility straight away. How could she not when it smote her in the face. She went

134

on, faltering: 'I was just saying to Ed. . . . In fact, I was wondering. . . .'

But no more words were willing to risk their necks. She looked helplessly at Miriam.

'Edward,' Miriam said, 'I need your help indoors.'

Just that. Edward. She needed his help indoors. Then, slam! Her friend hadn't so much as glanced at her.

Unbelieving, she turned to Ed; appealed to the distortion of his face which wavered at her through the rain which seemed to have fallen on her lashes out of the cloudless sky of a perfect afternoon.

Briefly, he touched her arm, wanted to get past.

'Goodbye; and thank you for. . . .'

A quick, sad flash of the old Ed. It burst out of her then: 'But what have I done?'

He didn't answer – appeared to be about to, but didn't.

'You know I wouldn't deliberately hurt. . . .'

'I know you wouldn't, not deliberately; and so does Miriam. But she's had a lot to put up with lately, too much provocation, unkindness. . . . It's been a strain on her.'

Harry Thornby! Of course. She said quickly: 'Ed, I did my best to stop. . . .'

'Yes. You meant well, Eva; you always do mean well. And don't think we haven't appreciated your friendship. But you oughtn't to have laughed at him, made him look small. What did you expect to happen except revenge?'

'Ed . . .' she began, puzzled.

'And it didn't bring you any luck, either, did it, Eva?'

A quick squeeze of the arm and he was past her, in his porch.

But she hadn't laughed at Harry. And what didn't bring her any luck? *Luck?*

A raised hand, a nod, the wraith of a smile; then he was inside his own house, the door shut against her.

Soon be home, Pussy. . . .

It was nearly midnight and the last bus had gone. She had reached The Avenue. Not far now. Not all that far. Not so far as you'd notice.

Old Road. Now that really was almost home. How many lamp-posts . . .? Come on, Eva, count them; it'll help the feet move forward.

She forgot to count them all the same. Alec and Jack Thornby, Ed and Miriam, Alec. . . . It was like a record which couldn't be switched off, a record with the stylus stuck in the same old groove.

In the end, worn out, she'd gone to the cinema and, wadded in like a chocolate, had fallen asleep. She'd slept through the final programme and awoken ravenous; and even though, when it came to it, she wasn't quite so hungry as she'd imagined, she forced herself to swallow those dry bites of sandwich, drink a glass of cheap red wine.

All of which had been good for her, and she acknowledged it. It was a step towards making life ordinary again; and if she hadn't yet got her bounce back – and she hadn't – she could at least believe that it would eventually return, even that it was a not abnormal condition, bounce.

Which was not a lot but it was something; something to be built on.

And one builds, she instructed Pussy, by being a dumpling; by having a diet of dumpling thoughts.

Nearly at the end of Old Road now. Nearly home, so keep going.

She kept going. Hollow, her feet echoed past crouching, shut-faced houses. . . .

Correction, Pussy. Eva Wootton walked down the street. Remember dumplings, prithee. State it in prose.

Prose. Dumplings. So she considered the need to replace her kitchen curtains. She must buy fabric and then – oh God! – actually sit down and make them. Well, she could. It would be that magic specific, something to do with her hands, which Doris Cope had recommended – see, Pussy, a dumpling thought!

She turned the corner into Barnes Farm Close.

Eva stopped, confused, like a moth trapped in lamplight. But it was Barnes Farm Close. Number one, hers; number three, the Johnsons'. She walked past her own – in spite of what, in that shocked moment, she saw – and examined theirs. *HOUSE FOR SALE*.

House for sale? *House* for sale? The Johnsons'?

The black sockets of the windows were blank. She'd spoken to Ed that afternoon, seen Miriam; but they'd already gone.

And then there was her own house. She stationed herself before it. A spray-gun, of course. Of course. Quick, for an easy getaway. Had the curtains opposite twitched to witness this among all those other things which the hidden eyes had so avidly taken in? And without protest, without neighbourly regret?

She read the words a second time, a third. Spelling correct, punctuation beyond reproach. Ten out of ten. No illiteracy here other than illiteracy of the heart. It was no more than the compliments of the season, Tigby style.

NIGGER-LOVER, GO!

Nigger-lover? *Nigger?* They meant that civilised man, Ed, that warm and vital woman, Miriam?

She found she could no longer feel anything. She felt nothing at all.

17

Eva had seen Alec's house once – by spying on it.

Why? A mixture of motives. Curiosity, of course. Also to have a setting; a place she'd be able to recall as she said to herself, he's home. Yes, and to catch a glimpse, if she could, of his children. Above all, to see his children.

So she'd gone out on a day excursion, like any Sunday tripper, to Hammel-on-Sea.

Still in her wrap that Thursday morning. Eva smiled to remember how, at the last minute, she'd lost her nerve and purchased a disguise from a kiosk on the beach – a florid headscarf and dark glasses with diamanté frames. But they made her look different all right, not Eva at all, and that gave her confidence to advance, though by a roundabout route, on Alec's house.

She knew exactly where the house was situated. She'd made it her business to find out: for it absorbed her, this passion to know about Alec and his life. Even its trivia were of interest – the colour of the front door; which way the staircase curved up from the hall.

It was a fine day in May, a May as golden as this one and her first in Tigby. On leaving the station she set out along the beach road where she passed an ice-cream parlour, two cafés, a fish and chip restaurant and a tired corner shop full of buckets, spades and faded postcards. Such visitors as the sunshine had lured to Hammel were clustered on the few hundred yards of sand within reach of these amenities, and she soon left them behind; and where the beach road curved away from the shore she saw the row of tamarisks Alec had described. Beyond them was the track over the dunes from which one could see the back of his house. On fine mornings he walked to the station along that track.

Cautious now, on the alert, counting the houses . . . then she was looking up a long lawn to a large white cottage whose windows and doors were open to the garden and the shore, just as he'd described it.

And there in the garden was Alec.

His back was to her. It seemed he'd just finished mowing the lawn and was stooping to switch off the motor. He straightened up and shouted something – she couldn't hear what – as he gestured towards the house; then, leaving the mower where it was, he ambled across to flop down in a canvas chair which stood under the oaks on the wind-razed side of the garden.

She dropped quickly down, her heart in a tumult, and watched from behind a tussocky hillock, her cheek scratched by the dune grass. Acid-sharp, she could see them still, those coarse spikes which had pushed up through the drifted sand.

A woman came out of the house, Jean. A large, laughing photograph of Jean stood on Alec's desk; she saw it every day when she took shorthand from him, had seen it every day in Garchester. Once, when he wasn't looking, she'd made a face at it – childish, of course, but there it was. And now here was Jean, the woman. Eva felt sick. She thought she'd assessed every hazard before setting out. What she hadn't reckoned on was how much more painful than the photograph the reality of Jean would be.

Yet now she was here she had to watch. Had to? Had to.

Jean had brought Alec his tobacco and pipe and was teasing him with them, holding them just out of reach, laughing, as in the photograph. Then snatch! He had them. Which was another jolt, for how well she knew it, that greedy, long-armed grab. It was the way he grabbed her.

Jean sank down on the grass then, arms looped loosely round her knees, smiling up at him while, leisurely, apparently content, he filled and lit his pipe. Unhappy? Deprived? She didn't look either, that wife of his. Even though Alec no longer made love to her; even though they hadn't shared a room since that first Christmas in Tigby. So was that what she'd come to Hammel to see, a man and woman at peace with each other – her man, Eva's?

No. But however much it hurt, as she knew it would, she did want to see those children.

She knew little about his children. Apart from the occasional remark, such as mentioning that they were with their grandparents, Alec rarely talked about them to her. But that reticence, she guessed, was to save her pain. So as not to remind her that he had once shared with Jean what was now hers alone. So as not to stab her with the fact that she would never bear him children herself. Because even then she was too old, ten years ago, at fifty.

It was sensitive of Alec, endearing – unlike his attitude to the photograph. It was expected, he said, that one should have one's wife's photograph on one's desk. It meant absolutely nothing.

It meant a lot to her.

And now here was the flesh and blood Jean resting against his knees, smiling into his face, owning him. And young enough still to bear him another child if by chance. . . .

Eva gave up then. Pressing her fists into her eyes, her forehead into the sand, she wept wild, unreasonable tears.

Unreasonable? Yes, they were unreasonable. She hadn't been deceived. Alec had been straight with her. He'd never complained that his wife misunderstood him, had never pretended he was unhappy with Jean, so today should have been no revelation. What he had

140

said was that he loved her, Eva, more; that since the move he and Jean had had separate rooms; that it was his duty to his children, that alone, nothing but his sense of the vulnerability of his children which made it impossible for him to break with their mother yet.

So, yes, her tears were foolish. Jean was ten years younger than she was, and beautiful; nevertheless, she had Alec's love and against that certainty the rest was unimportant.

All the same she'd lain there, lost among tufts of rank grass; had shut her eyes against the light and wished not to be.

When at last she sat up the sun was low. The mower had gone, she saw, and the chair; and they'd gone, too, Alec and his wife. She imagined them having supper casually from a tray before settling down in easy intimacy, perhaps to finish the crossword, or read a library book or watch television. Or perhaps they were going out – together, a couple – for a meal with friends. Or Alec might have his briefcase open – perhaps he had. Had he yet checked the schedules she'd reminded him about? He might be doing it now. He could, at that very moment, be scribbling notes for the report she would have to type tomorrow.

Eva stared at the white cottage which sprawled, a harmonious accretion of three centuries, across the top of the garden. So this was his home. This was the house to which she'd been invited for tea, urged to drop in for a drink, bidden to bring her face to have a name put to it. This was the house – or so she'd thought before that job in the North cropped up – where, one day, it could be she who sat on the grass laughing up into her husband's face.

But, above all, it was his children she'd hoped to see, those extensions of Alec, that responsible need which kept him anchored to Jean. Besides – and, yes, it had happened; she must be straight with herself – when she'd seen Alec to be weak or suspected his motives, she'd held on to this knowledge, a sure foundation for

141

trust. Alec might be a flawed human being, as fallible as the rest, but he would not risk damaging his children; his priorities were sound.

And the children weren't there. Were they with their grandparents again as they had been the weekend of the office dance? It was possible. But how like her bad luck to miss them. For this must be the only time; she must never spy on Alec again.

She'd walked back, far out, by the edge of the retreating tide, gone barefoot through the shallow ripples, giving herself over to their chill and to the ribbed sand under her feet. And there, still within sight of the house, she'd found the lump of driftwood.

Vividly, she recalled picking it up, balancing it on her hand, holding it like an hour-glass. She'd stared at it, that piece of wood which now held down her bills, trying to pin the moment in her mind and preserve for ever the meaning with which it was now invested.

But what meaning was that? What was it she'd sought to impress on herself with so much ceremony? That this was a souvenir of the day she'd dressed up – yes, and vulgarly – to spy on Alec? Or that Eva Wootton and the driftwood were one?

18

There had been no post on Thursday, nor was there any on Friday; and still no news of Nora's letter, about which she'd begun to give up hope; but under the *Tigby Argus* which lay on her mat Eva found a manila envelope, hand-delivered, addressed in block capitals to herself. The word *Miss* was heavily underlined. She raised her brows at that.

Ye have ploughed wickedness, ye have reaped iniquity. Daniel, X, 13.

Not a note, but a grubby square of printed card embellished by an ill-designed lily; the kind of thing which, in her childhood, her Sunday-school teacher had handed out as a reward for attendance. And sent anonymously. Of course.

All the same, she told Pussy, the prophet Daniel makes better reading than Win a Dream Home.

Which brought her back to the injunction sprayed on her own house. Sooner or later she'd have to do something about that mess; like ring the assurance company, like start collecting estimates. Meanwhile, it didn't trouble her. Meanwhile, it was there for all to see.

Suddenly curious, she went into her front room and stood, concealed by her curtains. Twenty-eight turned heads in the space of seven minutes; and she studied them, those people who had made occasion to walk past her house up a road which was normally empty at this time on a Friday morning. Some glanced, then hurried on; the majority slackened their pace to stare. One couple even stopped to lean on her gate like familiar friends come to pass the time of day while she gardened. They appeared to be discussing something in detail – her ploughing of wickedness? – and as they looked from number one to number three and back from number three to number one they were not, so far as she could tell, unduly displeased with what they saw. When, finally, they did move on it was with lingering glances; reluctant, it seemed, to go; afraid of missing something. So perhaps they weren't really going at all. Perhaps they'd merely gone off for deckchairs and a picnic before settling down in comfort in front of this house whose windows they'd scanned so hungrily, waiting for more iniquity to be reaped.

Twenty-eight. And not one had come to the door to offer help. Still, be fair, Pussy, she countered. Would I have walked up this path under the eyes of all the neighbours, rung this bell, stuck out my neck for someone who, after all, might be a criminal lunatic?

Would she? Eva pondered it. Well, yes, she would. It wouldn't have occurred to her to do anything else. So was this another of those things they meant when they said she didn't live in the same world as other people? She gave it up.

Which reminded her of another thing. She'd intended to get hold of Harry, to take him by the scruff of the neck if necessary, and force him to apologise to the Johnsons, make some kind of restitution, and now it was too late. So often, it seemed, things dawned on her too late.

It occurred to Eva then, though without anger, that it could have been Harry who'd defaced her walls. Was it? She wondered, with a sudden spurt of pity for the boy, whether this wasn't even a misguided gesture of filial piety to the father he'd disappointed, a belated attempt to make amends; for Harry, surely, would have heard how she'd humiliated his father, yes, and in front of those symbols of hate and fear which he called niggers. Poor ignorant, untaught boy!

It seemed to be turning into a week for backward looks.

Or was it broken ends? And, taken as a whole, her life, how many broken ends there were. She hadn't seen it quite this way before, but she recognised the truth now without surprise. Take, for example, that broken end, Ian's death.

It astonished her to recall, which she rarely did, that young Eva Wootton had once been married to a man called Ian South. But she had; and, if Ian had lived, today – today, good God! – would have been their ruby wedding anniversary. Yet it was doubtful if she'd have remembered even that fact had this not turned into a week for backward looks.

At the time, though, how traumatic it had been, that particular breaking-off. Ian was twenty-five and apparently strong. She'd had no premonition of disaster, there had been no sign to warn them, no hint that they should treasure each second which remained of an eight-month-old marriage. And then one night, in sleep, Ian's heart fell silent like an unwound clock.

She'd been shocked into an iceberg, and the ice had stayed with her. This, it seemed, was something she'd never surmount. The idea of another man was intolerable; and, sheathed in that ice, her child-bearing days had passed her by. Yet, if she was honest, this wasn't out of grief, though her grief was genuine. It wasn't even out of love of Ian, though she'd been fond of him and they'd been happy together in an unadventurous kind of way; and, though the shock of his death had been a nightmare, it had churned up nothing like the sick and mountainous waves Alec could raise in her; and in time even that shock had diminished, skins grown over the wound.

No, it wasn't love or mourning for Ian which had turned her into a woman alone. It was, she supposed, a kind of rage. For Ian's death – wasn't that yet another rejection? Irrational, yes, but that's the way it felt; and so bitterly did she feel it that, in a gesture of independence, a muddled I'll-show-you directed with equal vindictiveness towards a living God and a dead husband,

145

she'd reverted to the name of Wootton and taken to calling herself 'miss' again.

For this rejection, Ian's, stood too painfully on the scar of that prime wound which had never properly healed. Because who was she, this woman people called Eva?

Eva moved restlessly back to the window. As if to match her broken ends the weather, too, had broken up. Still at the window, she watched anchored leaves straining before the wind and all the planes they strove to move in.

Who was her mother? She'd often wondered. What kind of woman? And her father? Had he actually loved this woman who'd borne his child? Where were their roots, what their history, and what had gone wrong between them – apart from the presumably unwelcome fact of herself? It would seem there was no trace. Left on a doorstep in Dublin was the nearest she could get. Left on a doorstep, that of her adoptive mother, Nora's oldest friend.

The presumably unwelcome fact of herself.

Eva turned away at last and went back into the kitchen. It was her favourite place in this unloved stopgap of a house, meanly conceived though it was; and this was her favourite attitude, mooning with her elbows on the kitchen table. Perhaps her mother had been a skivvy – would that account for it? It wouldn't trouble her now what her mother had been, but it would have helped to know.

And what of her parents on this particular Friday in May? Were they both dead? Perhaps. Did either still live? It was always possible.

When she was a child she believed that she'd been stolen by tinkers from some grand house, then abandoned because she was a trouble to them; that somewhere in a nursery shrine her real parents wept, inconsolable. The woman she called Mother had laughed at this, had told her not to give herself airs and that she'd been wrapped in nothing but a moth-eaten bit of an old shawl. But, as Eva knew, the tinkers would have kept her satin robe, of course they would.

Later, a harsher fantasy took over. She was the child of some casual accident. Perhaps her mother was a prostitute – why not? That wasn't where the bitterness lay. But her mother was also human, with ordinary human choices; and her choice had been to dump her child on a doorstep like a pint of milk. Did she even know that her name was Eva or guess that she loved to dance?

And now – oh, just to know the truth, to get in touch! For how desperate she must have been, that poor mother of hers, to do a thing like that! Eva longed to comfort her, to tell her that it didn't matter any more, that she wasn't to grieve – for how could she not grieve, if only in secret? – and to be unable to do this was a second deprivation. And how insecure it made one, deprivation; how it made one cling.

Out of the blue a memory of childhood came back – herself at school, no more than six, holding a small square of white canvas and a needle threaded with wool. In a tin lid on her desk there were some beads – bright, glassy; they filled her with happiness – and she was to sew these beads on to the canvas in a straight line with no more than a single back-stitch behind each bead to keep it secure. A single stitch – did she understand? Yes, she understood. But the beads were so heavy, the wool so thin. What if the wool broke and the beads rolled all over the floor? What if she lost one? So, secretively, she'd sewn each bead over and over again, lashing it with clogged wool to the puckering canvas so that it would be safe. For that, to her, was what mattered most; that she shouldn't lose it, that it should be secure.

But it turned out that, yet again, she'd been wicked. Scolding and snipping like a frenzied bird, Miss Chapman had attacked the tangle of threads and dropped the beads one by one back into the tin to be given – a present – to a more obedient child while Eva was left with her hands on her head to contemplate misfortune's face.

That so trivial a memory should, like the other, carry such a load of grief.

And still no kettle. And still no news of Nora's letter, though she'd telephoned to ask a number of times. Eva refilled the small saucepan, thinking of Nora; brooded over it while minute bubbles gathered and silvered as the water heated up.

She could remember Nora right back to the shadows in which stood a cot with a drop side and a teddy bear; a high chair with a hole in the seat through which, astonishingly, one sometimes discovered that one had excreted; the time of first noticing how strange the word 'string' sounded and of being stung by a bee when she tried to kiss it.

In those days it had been Auntie Nora O'Hara who was always in and out of their house, for she and the Woottons were very close. Only much later had Nora gone off to marry Pringle. Why had she left him? Eva knew no more than Nora had chosen to tell, and had never thought to ask; in fact had had little interest in knowing more till now, and now it was too late. Would the letter have told her?

And the Woottons – that was too late, too. Her mother might have given her away, but they'd kept her, those Woottons with whom, even now, she was so childishly dissatisfied. They'd made her their own as best they knew how, and brought her to England with them when they moved – and wasn't that a marvellous thing to do for a foundling wrapped in nothing but a moth-eaten bit of an old shawl? But blinded by her hunger for identity she'd never seen it like that before; and, humbled now, she felt small in herself as she recalled her grudging obedience, her lack of love. Yet without the Woottons she would never have had Nora, and what a deprivation that would have been, yet another.

Needs – what treacherous things they were.

She'd been fond of that mischievous, exuberant woman from the start; and Nora had made no secret of the fact that she doted on her, awkward and unsentimental though that doting might be. And, imperceptibly at first, later imperiously, it was, as she grew old, to Eva that Nora turned for support. All the same, it wasn't just out of old acquaintance that Nora chose to live with her when she no longer cared to be on her own, for – as she admitted with some glee – no one else would have her. Or nobody she'd soil her tongue by asking; as tart as ever she told Eva; and knowing the relish Nora took in what she called bein'-meself-and-to-hell-wid-the-lot-of-thim Eva could well believe it.

Then who on earth could that relative be? Hardly one of Pringle's. And had he made Nora unwelcome, or hadn't she wished to soil her tongue by asking? Would the letter have told her that, too?

How typical of Nora to leave a mystery! She'd always been secretive; but to have a relation, her only one, and not to say a word in all those years!

A mug of tea in her hand, Eva stood for a while staring through the side window. The sky was still in tumult, a William Blake sky, layered, mysterious. From a sky like that God could descend in majesty with all His angels. Or it might merely rain.

The dining room: poetry, drama, language reference books. . . . She went back to the kitchen, through to the hall.

She'd never liked this house, would never have taken this house given time and a choice; but it was available when she needed a house, and what was it, after all, but a stopgap? Amazing that Doris should actually fancy this stopgap of a house.

That third stair. . . .

Back to the kitchen again. Perhaps that unknown mother had indeed been a skivvy. Perhaps she had kitchen writ large in her genes – a chromosome designed for the programming of Eva: Get thee to a kitchen! And what a room; a mere Oxo cube. But she'd settled for it. Because it wouldn't be long now before things came to a head.

149

Ten years ago – nearly ten and a half.

In the garden, so close together that she could take them in at a glance, were the wych-elm and the Christmas tree, the living and the dead. What if she'd chosen differently? What if she'd gone to London as she'd planned?

These curtains which had outlived their usefulness had been stopgaps, too, run up that first weekend from a pair she'd brought from Nora's old room in Garchester. For what was the point of buying new ones when these would do for the next few months, for as long as she was here?

Garchester. It had an alien ring now. She might just as well have said Persepolis. Yet she'd been married in Garchester, and Ian was buried there. It was to Garchester that Nora had come when, imperious, she'd elected to live with her. She'd first met Alec in Garchester; and, yes, it was in Garchester that she'd worked so hard, so unbelievably more than hard, to achieve that triumph which, because of him, her obsession, Alec, she'd finally thrown away.

Facts, all of them. And they didn't weather or mutate with time, facts like that; weren't subject to changes of mood. They remained what they were: facts, knobbly, intractable.

Eva examined the curtains. A hem had come undone and when she pulled at the thread it broke, rotten, in her hand. But under the fold of that hem, vivid and unfaded, she came on the pattern as it had been in Garchester two decades before.

Did Alec realise, even dimly, what she'd given up? Almost certainly not, but whose fault was that?

But, God, the work! The sheer grind of it! To go back to school at forty with nothing but her shorthand, typing and office management certificates and start aiming for university entrance. . . . It had been like setting out to dig up an allotment with a teaspoon.

Life and the tricks it plays. She'd been widowed for twenty years before she discovered, and then by chance, that there were other choices – yes, even for an ordinary person like herself.

The Chief had passed on a ticket he couldn't use and it had come down to her; and for no other reason than that she didn't know how to get out of accepting it she'd gone to a lecture on English lyric poetry by a Dr Idris Owen Lloyd.

She'd expected to be bored, out of her depth; but she emerged feeling like Saul smitten by light on the road to Damascus. Had life, then, this other dimension, an air that felt like home?

She'd waited for him in the foyer. She wanted to be his student. How should she go about it?

The innocent cheek of the woman! His student? It was months before she discovered that Dr Lloyd taught only one non-university course, his scholarship-level élite.

But Idris hadn't treated it as cheek; hadn't dismissed her, though careful from the start that she should see things straight. There were no short cuts, and he told her so. She'd have to begin at the bottom. And how did she, in middle age, feel about starting at the bottom, eh?

She wanted to join his class.

Had she any 'O' Levels – School Cert as was?

No.

Not even one?

Not even one. She'd left school too early.

Kindly then, gently, and late as it was, the caretaker rattling his keys at them, he'd led her to see just where it lay, that bottom at which she'd have to begin, and how formidable the task she so lightly proposed to undertake.

Formidable, perhaps; but he didn't say impossible. She pointed this out to him. They assessed each other.

'Well, Miss Wootton?'

'When can I join your evening class, Dr Lloyd?'

Stubborn – of course; and ignorant as hell.

'Well. . . . But first you must get yourself a few good

151

'O' Levels. Pick up at least one more language – take on French, but Latin would be an advantage, too, if you're hoping to work with an old-fashioned chap like me. And history – that's essential. But, above all, read Miss Wootton, *read*! If you can come back to me in a few years' time with that behind you and a good grade for language and literature, I promise I'll teach you myself even if I have to do it in my spare time. And if I teach you, Miss Wootton. . . .' Confident, as he had a right to be. 'And if you can stand it. . . .'

'Thank you, Dr Lloyd. But what shall I read?'

As simple as that: what shall I read?

She could pick up a reading list from his office on Monday evening. And – beaming, sardonic – the best of luck!

She picked it up. It was seventeen pages long. *Seventeen pages!* She hadn't known there were so many books in the world, but he'd headed it: *Essential Basic Reading*. On top of which she was to learn French, Latin, history – to name, as Bert would say, but a few. On top of which she was forty and with Nora that same week deciding to live with her; Nora proclaiming that she was an old woman now, wisha, and needing to be cared for, helpless as she was, God love us!

But there was something else in that envelope along with the reading list – the first *Golden Treasury*, Palgrave's, with the compliments of Dr Lloyd, a present. Typically, he had scribbled a warning at the bottom of the printed slip: *Enjoy but beware; not definitive. Omissions include John Donne (1572–1631) pronounced 'dun' as in 'cow'. A scandal! Look for others and tell me. I.O.L.*

She had never owned a poetry-book before.

Idris hadn't believed she'd stick it, and she wasn't too sure herself; but when they ran into each other and he asked how she was doing, fine, she'd lie, just fine.

But she did stick it; and, amazingly, Nora was wild with delight when she outlined the project and hinted at what it might mean; and, unpredictable, chameleon as Nora might be, she never faltered in this. The tired, hard-done-by old lady who'd come to be cherished – who'd come determined to be cherished – changed overnight. It was Nora now who took the initiative, Nora who did the cherishing, leaving Eva free to study once the day's work was done.

That study became an obsession as, later, Alec became an obsession. Never mind all those hours in the lecture room at the end of a tough day. Never mind falling asleep over her books at two in the morning. Never mind those dead weekends. Never mind all those subjects – French, for instance – with which she had to come to terms.

Eva smiled down at the broken end of cotton as she recalled the panic with which French had filled her.

But she'd mastered even French. Inch by inch she'd struggled up the cliff face, afraid to look up, not daring to look back, intent only on the nearest hand hold, the next small target, this week's minuscule success.

Then suddenly – sunlight. She was up that vertiginous slope and looking about her. Not there yet, not where she intended to be, not by any means; but already dancing where she'd limped, seeing where she had been blind. She had the capacity, she knew she could do it; that was the point. And so, by now, did Idris Lloyd.

In the event she got nine good 'O' Levels – nine, for God's sake! Excessive as always, unconfident as always, just to make sure. Those beads, Pussy, those bloody beads!

It took her seven years to get there, but she was in Idris Lloyd's 'S' Level group at last.

Eva found herself back in the dining room. Hardy, Herrick, Hobdell, Homer. . . . she drew out the Bridges edition of Gerard Manley Hopkins, opened it at random.

O the mind, mind has mountains; cliffs of fall. . . .

Snapped it shut. Thrust it back. A woman's place is in the kitchen.

Yet poetry had been her passion. They tossed

153

quotations at each other, he and she – in the canteen, passing on the stairs. . . . Once across a crowded Woolworth on Christmas Eve, her arms full of holly. When it was reported back to her that Dr Lloyd considered Eva Wootton ample reward for a lifetime of mediocrity she cried herself to sleep for joy.

How hard he was with her, now that she was succeeding. He challenged every statement, forced her to fight her corner, to produce her evidence, to say with greater austerity and precision what she'd imagined was clear in the first place – which, as he was enchanted to demonstrate, had not been so. (Drunk on duty again, I see, Miss Wootton. How often must I remind you that words are strong ale?)

And, he informed her, autocratic as always, when she had her good 'A' Levels for French and Latin – as he was reliably informed was likely – and her 'S' for English Language and Literature – as she'd better – she was to read for an honours degree, so she should start applying for a place now. He advised London. UCCA forms. . . . *Job?* What job? Oh, but she must give that up! *This* was to be her job – and money would, of course, be what was known as forthcoming. An interesting circumlocution, was it not? Parthenocarpy? Parthenogenesis? Which did she . . .? *She dared to stand there and tell him she didn't know the words?* Then, look them up, woman, look them up! And London, yes. She must flee the minnows of the Garchester pond, find the open sea – or *the deep* as, no doubt, she would put it when carried away. Yes? He despaired of her. All the same, it wasn't too early (a tossed aside) to begin thinking in general terms about the possibility of a doctoral study. . . .

Those last swirling months! Forms, interviews, revision – a year's leave mortgaged for that; yes, and those last-minute panics, too, the tears of exhaustion. With Nora alone calm. Nora strong. Nora thinking for her when she, Eva, was past knowing which day of the week it was let alone the hour. How grateful she'd been then to this old lady – this now astonishingly vigorous old lady – who, thank God, hadn't chosen to soil her tongue by asking anyone else to take her in.

When suddenly, without applying for it, she was offered promotion. The head of Sites and Buildings had, apparently, had his eye on her.

Dishy Mr Burroughs! Without even trying she'd netted one of the most prized jobs in the Town Hall. Wasn't she lucky!

Wasn't she. The world her oyster. All this and Alec, too.

The hall once more – that damned third stair! So that's where she'd put the apples on – what? Wednesday, was it? Well, they might as well stay, like the words sprayed on her wall proclaiming that the Johnsons had once been her friends. Yet what a service that vandal had done her. Misery suspended, floating over but not in that black hole, she was anaesthetised. God moving in His mysterious way again, no doubt. Not anaesthetised against Idris, though, nor G.M. Hopkins; and as for that third stair, as for the telephone which wouldn't ring. . . . Could he be ill, Alec? Had he perhaps had an accident? If only she knew.

Well, you don't, she told herself, so move on and merrily hent whatever it is.

So into the front room – aha! Who are these coming to the sacrifice? Ode on a Tigby Urn, she informed Pussy. Mr Keats.

There was quite a crowd in front of her gate. One of the women carried a young child who was licking an ice cream and there was a man taking photographs of her house. She lifted the curtain to look at him and, animated at first, the group was suddenly still – a frieze, and not unbeautiful.

Eva shrugged and turned away. She was scarcely in the kitchen when the doorbell rang. Her heart quickened painfully. Was someone sorry for her, then? Had she a genuine neighbour after all?

When the bell rang again Eva went back to the door.

Her hand was already on the key. But all those faces lined up, waiting for her, gloating. . . .

'Who is it?'

'Miss Wootton? Miss Eva Wootton?'

She didn't recognise the voice – a man's, ordinary. Nothing either for or against it, that voice.

'Yes?'

'I've come as a friend. . . .'

As a friend? Why not just be one, man of goodwill?

'Who are you?'

'If you'll open your door for one minute. . . .'

'Why?'

A real Tigby clout, that's why. Break your arm it could, Pussy. Like a swan's wing. Or so they say.

'I'd appreciate a word in private. . . .'

In private? With that mob there? She slipped back to the front window, and a glance showed her all she needed to know. The photographer was missing. Press. Of course.

What a pity. She hadn't seen anyone – not what you could call anyone – for two days. She'd have liked a chat.

After a while the ringing of the doorbell stopped. From the telephone there was still no sound.

19

Lucky? She examined the word, rejected it. Yet what word was there to describe that particular cataclysm, the miraculous disaster which chance had tossed into her lap?

There wasn't one. With Alec she felt herself to be a woman again. With Alec she became a woman again. How describe that?

How did it come about? She'd no idea. Only that the igloo she'd inhabited for so many years was melting round her, that the voice of the turtle was heard in the land.

Her future was already charted, secure; and, clearly, Alec Burroughs had planned his, too. She'd seen from the start that he was hungry for the top and would be charmingly ruthless about getting there. Alec, who, in any case, was married to somebody called Jean. She'd observed the photograph. One couldn't miss it.

Each had a life of his/her own which would go on as before, for one does not lightly set plans like his and hers aside. That agreeable unease which was accommodating itself within her could have no part in that life, and she knew it. She saw their futures, separate, different. Well, then?

Well, then, she fell in love all the same.

It was a delicate, a fragile beginning, that first post-winter shoot; nothing to be recognised as love. No more, to begin with, than a heightened pleasure in being alive; a belief that the day was brighter than others seemed to find it. Within, she sensed a subtle change in the balance of flesh and spirit, with spirit uppermost yet, oddly, clay needing to be decked out to best advantage. For the first time in years she took pleasure in buying herself new clothes.

But, above all, there was this aeration of bliss; and with Alec to serve – to be allowed to serve – what more could she ask? Her days dazzled her. Food was suddenly too coarse for this vibrant joy. Her spirit sang, her flesh rejoiced at being recalled to life. Daily she larded Alec with blessings, and he knew nothing about it. In the beginning it was even part of her pleasure that he knew nothing about it.

She'd never known love like this, never guessed at it. She kept it to herself, this secret, and it blazed out of her.

She looked marvellous, the girls exclaimed; she'd lost pounds! Was it a diet? Exercise? Had she been to a sauna? A health farm? Taken up yoga? Was she into TM? For how on earth . . .!

No way on earth. That fragile shoot had devoured her. A sturdy vine now, full of light, it had made her anew in its own image.

She smiled and thanked the girls – what else to say?

But she must have given up *something* . . .!

Oh, well, butter, perhaps; dairy foods – that kind of thing.

That kind of thing.

They became lovers almost by accident.

She'd stayed on late at the office to finish typing a report, and he took her out to dinner. Jean was away for the week. And so it was. But lightly, a pleasure. A moment to be enjoyed like the bottle of wine they'd shared. Nothing to be intense about.

Eva let it happen. Accepted it with wonder. But afterwards. . . . No more to him than pleasure, then, this thing which she felt to be worship and grace? And lightly? Had she ever in her life taken anything lightly?

Before the week was out he came back to her. When he asked for a stone her arms, full of abundance, heaped him with bread. But if all a man wants is a stone, a moment of pleasure as lightly taken as a glass of wine, what was her bread but an embarrassment? She felt degraded. Could such sweet, such bitter fruit grow on the same vine?

Such sweet, such bitter fruit; and on the same vine.

Meanwhile there was that future of hers – the good degree which would make a chance of doctoral work possible. It was only a matter of time now, Idris insisted; that, and of letting nothing else get in the way. Why had he said that? Had he, too, noticed something? Or was it no more than an item of that pastoral care which he lavished so generously on all his students?

But it pulled Eva up, forced her to face the immediate alternatives. Ruthlessly, she outlined them to herself. Alec didn't love her – no, she must face it, it was a fact – so she could either break it off now, herself, make a clean end; or she could enjoy such limited-term benefits as Alec might choose to offer until the time came for her to go and get on with her own life.

She was immediately appalled. Break it off? What kind of choice was that? Just as soon ask her to cut her throat. And get on with her own life? How could she if she'd broken it off?

And she'd thought she'd gone into this with her eyes open!

The results came towards the end of August – a triumphant 'S' for Language and Literature and three very good 'A' Levels – beads, Pussy, beads!

Nora was in raptures. Always volatile, Eva had never known her higher. It was no surprise to Nora. She'd realised Evie had it in her. There was good blood there – bloody good blood, Nora insisted. Eva let her carry on, though the words depressed her. For whose blood was it that was so bloody good? Whose child had gained these laurels?

They both got very drunk.

A glowing card came from Dr Lloyd along with a

159

particular lexicon she'd been lusting after. *For Eva* – the Wootton fallen away – *with affection and respect – admiration understood. Idris.*

She had indeed arrived.

Eva decided to say nothing to Alec until confirmation came from London. As it would. It was only a matter of time.

Time? She was wary of the protean deceiver now. At what point in time had she encountered it, that moment after whose passing the privilege of being allowed to love was no longer enough; after which, with such desperate dependence, she needed to be loved in return? Needed to be loved – the treachery of needs!

She hadn't long to wait. The place was hers – everything, it seemed, was hers including an awesome award she hadn't even heard of. Money was indeed forthcoming. She could give up her job without fear; must tell Alec at once so that he could find someone to fill her place – secretarial understood.

She armed herself against him, prepared her face to confront him, Alec, who never read a book or what Idris would have called a book. So it wouldn't have done, would it, anyway?

Then she lost her nerve, had a sleepless night and had to prepare herself all over again.

She went in jaunty, grin pinned in place, flourishing her letter.

'You read that, mister!'

'What's all this about, you chirpy woman?'

He took it and casually began to skim; then, suddenly arrested, suddenly serious, he glanced at her.

'*Eva . . .!*'

He went back to the letter, and she watched the movement of his eyes; saw the care with which he weighed the words now, and that he read the letter through twice. Saw that his eyes were still fixed on the page when that page was at an end.

'*Well . . .!*'

He put the letter on his desk, smoothed it, looking

neither at her nor at her letter but at the space between himself and the words as he gathered himself together to congratulate her. She watched him arrange a smile for her as she'd arranged one for him. Had it so startled him, then, to learn that she had a life of her own, a bright future away from his? He looked shattered.

'This is magnificent, my dear!'

No tears, she'd warned; tears go with things like bread and commitment, not with glasses of wine. But how warm his voice was, and how she craved warmth. She hungered for it as she hungered for her roots, as though it could, that warmth, bestow an identity on her, make her whole.

He swam in her vision; was obscured as his arms went round her. And in the office! They'd agreed never that; as she tried to remind him, sniff sniff.

Bugger the office!

His hand was on the intercom switch. Joanna? I'm not to be disturbed, not for anybody. No, not even for him. I don't care if he is, put him off.

'Now, then, out with it, my love.'

His love – Alec's? It tumbled out of her: 'I don't know what to do . . .!'

But Alec knew. What she was going to do was let him take her home. She could tell him all about it then. They could talk things over properly. Joanna was instructed to cancel his meetings; and she, Eva, it was stated, had a migraine and was going back to bed. No connection.

Everything else thrust aside, they'd made love as though the world was about to end. And that was when he said it: 'I love you, Eva.'

No, it wasn't just sex, not any more. He loved her, he actually loved her. He'd said so at last. He volunteered the fact – but sadly, for wasn't she planning to go?

Thank God Nora was out of town for the day! That was the first time it occurred to her that Nora might sometimes be a liability.

They talked, they talked. . . . Her dilemma? What about his?

161

'Yes, darling, but. . . .' Troubled. Marvelling.

'But what?' he asked, then stopped her mouth with kisses.

One thing emerged, became clear; they must contrive to stay together. The only problem was the practical one – how?

Well, there was this job in Tigby, he was saying – a useful next step, actually; so if he decided to apply. . . .

It turned out that he had decided to apply. He'd been on the phone to friends there and they'd assured him he was sitting pretty.

Tigby? She was appalled. Right up in the Midlands? She nerved herself to say it: 'Alec, if you want to move. . . .'

'I need to move. One's too old too soon these days.'

'. . . Then, please go for something in London, eh? If you do that. . . .'

'I can't do that,' he told her, glum. 'I haven't the right contacts. I wouldn't stand an earthly.'

He took his arm away, made himself a little remote. They lay in silence and she shut her eyes, wretched.

'Do you mind so very much about Tigby?' she asked at last.

'I have to mind. My next move is all-important. For both of us. And Tigby's absolutely right.'

'For both of us? she said, confused.

Alec looked at her, hurt.

'I was going on the assumption that it mattered to you to stay with me; but if that isn't the case. . . .'

'Oh, *idiot*! But what am *I* to do?'

'I can't let you go, Eva, not now. I love you.'

'Do you?'

He put his arms round her again, held her close.

'Don't ever doubt that, my dear.'

It wasn't Alec she was at war with, it was herself; and in that particular civil war what chance had her solitary future in London?

So it was agreed that where he went she'd go, too. And initially as his secretary – he could fix that.

162

Because the personal side, Jean. . . . She did realise, didn't she, that he'd need a bit of time to sort things out, that it couldn't all happen overnight?

A bit of time, yes; but she hadn't known then about the children and what that would mean in terms of time.

The next day he applied for, and ultimately got, this job where he had friends at court – Jack Thornby, as she now realised, and Marty Pike; that gang. And she followed him. She fled the minnows of the Garchester pond and came to Tigby. How's that for the deep? she asked Pussy.

A bit of time. It had taken nine years for him to give even that firm commitment which – and not unreasonably, it seemed to her – she'd assumed from the start. But looking back now, spreading them out like coins on the palm of her hand, what did those golden words of his in Garchester amount to? No more than golden words. He loved her, yes; but he'd made no promise which she could legally have held him to had she been that kind of woman. And then a year ago, when she'd grown accustomed to waiting, he'd committed himself at last – yes, and without any pressure from her. What's more, he'd kept his word. He'd told Jean the truth and now he was a free man.

Oh, but if only he weren't so awkward! If only it were easier to be direct with him! If only he'd stop sulking about her absence, her letter, and *ring*! Until he did – that other dread apart, like believing the worst – she had this nagging fear that he was ill or had had an accident; that he could, even at this moment, be lying in some strange bed, delirious, calling for her as Nora had done.

If only Alec would ring and Nora's letter be retrieved the world might become solid in her view again, with bread and butter and five pee off a tin of peas a matter of at least mild interest once more.

But what did she mean, the worst? How anxiety revealed the vulgar wasteland in her mind! Or was it that too much had happened too quickly, as it had in Railway Terrace; that she'd had a traumatic week, was low, fanciful, not quite herself? The worst? When he'd given that firm commitment? That wasn't Alec's way. Awkward, yes; but awkwardness was another thing.

Eva stared down at her spread fingers as she tried to relive the joy which had flooded her, the confidence which his promise, explicit at last, had given. It had wounded her in their early days together, that measuring out of himself by the teaspoonful, the selective holding back. And, at the time, astonished her, too. She supposed, in love as she was, that she hadn't been capable of seeing him straight. Certainly she'd never bargained for calculation; had imagined him all fire and air.

All fire and air – Alec!

Not that she really wanted him any different from the way he was, her flesh and blood Alec with his own particular set of imperfections. Especially now that ambivalence was in the past. He'd declared himself; and now, as with so many things, it was only a matter of time.

And did it matter, except to her pride, that Jack Thornby had been instrumental in getting him that job in the North as he, or one of his kind, had also helped him to get a foothold in Tigby? She didn't like it – God, no; she resented it, wished it hadn't happened, but that wasn't the question. Was it *important*?

It was a question she dodged. Watched herself dodge.

Obliquely then the thought came to her how, in love, one so willingly accepted, so little examined, unacceptable data. That one pushed aside the barbed edge of truth, anxious to protect the hurtful loved one – yes, even to clearing briars from the path down which he was advancing to inflict pain. And all the time praying – *mindlessly* was the word that came to her – that he might never know the extent of the hurt or guess at the devastating total of the damage he'd done.

Was this what not living in the same world as other people meant? Or is it weakness of intellect, Pussy? I cried.

She was suddenly still as a pattern, glimpsed and already forgotten, seemed to fall into place. It was as though a missing bit of jigsaw had been under her fingers all the time.

Oh, stop it, she told Pussy wearily. Let's think about something else, eh?

That was the trouble with obsessions; there rarely was anything else.

20

Eva took the *Tigby Argus* up to bed. Bed was, on the whole, the most comfortable place besides being nearer the phone. She glanced at the headlines as she went.

UPROAR OVER NEW COUNTY HALL: '*A Shambles!' says Councillor Pike*.

She heard a voice say: 'That should make soothing bedtime reading.'

Below, in smaller type as clearly of less importance than the squandering of ratepayers' money: *Startling Increase in Vandalism*; and, insignificant, at the bottom of the page: *Unemployment Figures Rocket*.

It caught her eye then, the photograph top centre. Marty Pike, flanked by two ladies in long dresses showing much plump upper arm, beamed from the frame. Eva glanced at the caption. She stopped on mid-stair. Mrs Pike and Mrs Thornby, widow of. . . . But this was pink polyester, peach polyester, the women into whose eyes she'd looked with such contempt that lifetime ago.

Nora. She rang the bus station yet again, but the office was closed. If only Alec would ring!

The telephone rang.

Eva's mind seemed to turn a somersault, spring into space.

'Alec . . .!'

'Miss Wootton?' A woman's voice. 'Just a moment, please.'

Of course, his secretary. Hadn't she herself done this more times than she could remember? Oh, *Alec!* Joy exploded all about her head. Her arteries pumped champagne. Her diaphragm was brilliant with light.

'Your call's on the line.'

'Alec! Alec . . .!'

A man's voice in her ear. A persuasive voice, but not his.

'Who . . .?'

'. . . Sympathies . . . act of wanton vandalism . . . disgraceful disregard of property. . . .'

'Who am I speaking to?'

'*Tigby Argus*, Miss Wootton; Joe Grey here. Would you care to comment on the events which led up to . . .?'

She put the handset down on the bedspread. Muted by distance and fabric the voice clacked on. Eva sighed. Not too good, that champagne, now. Cana of Galilee in reverse, she told Pussy. Eau impotable.

'. . . Your next-door neighbours, I understand, have already left. . . .'

One pillow, two. She bunched them behind her, made herself comfortable.

'. . . But wouldn't you agree – how shall I put it? – that you enjoy being a little provocative . . .?'

Eva raised her brows. Was it Nora Joe Grey was describing? It sounded remarkably like Nora. She settled down with a kind of polite but bored attention to read the *Tigby Argus*.

The new County Hall. There was an account, not entirely accurate but near enough the truth to make uneasy reading for some, of the planning, the building and now, it would seem, the scandal of the new County Hall.

'Well, well!' she said, her attention engaged; for Salwart's Folly would be open to the public tomorrow morning.

She'd go. Why not? She had to do something. Yet what could she reasonably do with her time? Life had shrunk so small. Depressed, she imagined her days, unholdable as water, sliding through her fingers as the sand had slid when she lay out on the dunes below Alec's house willing the hours and her hurt to pass.

Hearing the dialling tone she hastened to replace the handset. Rather risk Joe Grey again than leave the phone off the hook.

So the Council was allowing a fascist rally – and on Council property – on Sunday afternoon. Quite a weekend. 'Wounded Soldier' was in indignant flood and 'Sabbatarian' (name and address supplied) in fine Old Testament flow.

Eva pressed doggedly on. Drains. Right of way through newlyweds' home. Missing granny found. Heartbreak kiddie smiles again. Butcher welcomes stay of execution. (Stay of *execution*, Pussy?)

Of course, the sensible thing would be to get a job; Peter Elliot was right about that. Any kind of job would do to tide her over – any kind, except Marty Pike's.

She ran her eye down the small ads picking out those muted cries for help disguised as three-piece suite, new, going cheap; and baby, thirteen months, no trouble.

Mature person required . . . ah! She read it again.

Mature person required as receptionist/secretary, afternoons and evenings, at prosperous country club. Knowledge of office practice an advantage. Generous fringe benefits – meaning the odd gin, my cat – *Salary according to suitability and experience* – the bargaining clause. *Apply in writing (recent photograph) or phone for appointment. Harriets, The Links, Tigby 2915.*

This was a job she could do standing on one ear. Correction: this was a non-job, etcetera.

Did she want it? No, she didn't. She thought of Idris. Was he, too, dead; or still alive and angry?

She found herself at the dressing table, Alec's card in her hand, a reminder that he was still in touch. How little one needed to keep the heart high, yet how deeply one needed that little. If only he'd ring, even briefly; just be there. And of course it couldn't have been his secretary. Like the bus station, his office would have closed hours ago.

Peering into the mirror she touched her hair, fluffed it up, tried to make the most of it. Age, age! Why did hair have to leave the head only to reappear, pale as straw, on the upper lip!

Did she want that job? Not want it, no; all the same, she crossed the room and rang Tigby 2915.

It was ridiculous. She couldn't justify it. There was no logical reason for her feeling; but a certainty was growing within her that this was what she had to do.

21

No post on Saturday except for the first three post-cards she'd sent Nora, readdressed without comment in Matron's precise hand.

But Bob rang the bell, although she'd left the milk money out; Bob not quite looking at her, speaking in a rush.

'My old lady says you're not to come to tea, Mrs Wootton.'

Tea? She remembered and nodded, relieved.

'She won't 'ave you in the 'ouse, that's what she says. Won't 'ave you in the 'ouse. She ain't 'aving no truck, she says, with wickedness and thingummy.'

A sly look; the prepared speech a little stumbled over. So it was Bob's mother who'd sent her the text; and delivered by Bob, as she wanted Eva to know. An old lady who knew better than to call her Mrs Wootton. Whose right to supplementary benefits had been pushed through by Jack Thornby. Who cut the cake Sundays.

'That's all right, Bob,' Eva said mildly. 'Goodbye.'

She refused to glance up or in any way acknowledge the crowd which was already gathering on the pavement. The crowd which would no doubt question Bob about her. And what would he say? That she'd ploughed wickedness and reaped thingummy? Or that she took four pints of milk a week?

She went back upstairs to get ready for her visit to the new County Hall.

Eva chose her plainest, quietest suit, the colour

called donkey. She grinned as she put it on. Some moke, that quiet, plain one, she told Pussy.

She'd already composed some plain but decidedly unquiet questions about the Folly and she intended to ask them in as public and forthright a manner as possible. Who'd be conducting the group? If only it could be Salwart himself; he'd deserve it for playing the gang's game, and, as a ratepayer, she'd let him have it, forget the other connection. She felt strong today, capable of taking on all comers. All the same, she hoped it wasn't Peter. But if it was she'd take him off for a drink afterwards – given he was still speaking to her, of course.

Eva was back in town!

She whistled a snaky little tune as she put out a dress to change into for the interview later; found the matching shoes, gloves, handbag. And very nice, too, Pussy. Most discreet. For a mature person hoping to attract fringe benefits, I mean.

But she'd no intention of being either mature or discreet this morning. She was setting out with the deliberate intention of putting the cat among the pigeons.

It made such a difference to life, it most certainly did, to have a structure for the day. And, on top of that, to have this serene feeling – it was still with her – that she was in harmony with whatever purpose there was for Eva, that this was what she must do. Odd, that, when she was going to demand to see Polly Arkwright's larder, the typing pool where the secretaries worked knee-hole to knee-hole under artificial light, the spacious members' dining room whose picture windows overlooked the wooded valley.

They got her photograph as she came through the gate. National press this time. Was the world, then, so short of disasters this week that they had to fall back on hers?

'Your views on South Africa, Miss Wootton. . . .?'

'Just turn your head an inch. . . . And *smile*, girlie! Front-page pic!'

'Full frontal if you like, but you'll have to co-operate!'

They didn't actually touch her. They didn't force her to do anything other than what she was already doing, which was to walk calmly away from them.

A young woman with a card urged her to take it.

'Ring this number. The woman's point of view. We'll make it worth your while.'

Cheers from the women, groans from the men.

Eva ignored the card, ignored the girl. Cheers from the men, groans from the women. Someone waved a Union Jack. It felt, confusedly, like being a pop star. Or a terrorist apprehended after a siege.

Wondering whether she ought to hold her hands above her head or get out her pen to sign autographs, Eva moved forward, and the wall of the idle, the curious, the sensation-seekers parted, if reluctantly, to let her through.

His face was bilious with anger. Eva tried to soothe him.

'It's not so bad as all that.'

'Louts, scandalmongers, the rubbish of society!'

'People,' she pointed out.

He looked at her like an old horse in a knacker's yard – that is, if one knew what an old horse in a knacker's yard looked like, which one could only guess. But that he should be sorry for her, Mr Locked-bolted-and-barred! And that he should have gone out of his way to say so!

He'd caught her up at the bus stop; had burst in on her calm without apology, for it was monstrous, he said, that scene at her gate.

But had he witnessed it from behind tweaked curtains, she wondered, side by side with his wife? What did it matter? His distress was genuine enough.

And now, having caught her up, he would not be shaken off. Where was Miss Wootton going? The new County Hall? Then, if she didn't mind, he'd accompany her, if only to save her from further indignity.

Eva was staggered afresh. Not only was he sorry for her, prepared not to judge her, he even knew who she was. It shamed her to realise how little effort she'd made to identify him.

His name, she discovered, was Gerry Smith. Gerry! Such a cheerful name for the man in the iron mask. But now that mask had gone. He wasn't talking easily, but with a kind of shy concern which won her over. He was like that brother which the child left on the doorstep had often longed to have.

'So you've retired from local government. . . .'

He knew that, too. The conductor eyed her, and two or three passengers turned their heads and whispered; but Gerry Smith sat on making small talk at her side. It was a brave gesture for a diffident man. Eva hoped that Tigby wouldn't make him pay for it.

They got off the bus at last and began to walk up the hill. He asked, apparently interested, why she'd wanted to come. It was, of course, an open day. . . .

She wanted to ask some awkward questions. People ought to *know*.

'Know what, Miss Wootton?'

'The truth.'

'Truth? To have the facts isn't the same as knowing the truth. Truth is something one appreciates from within.'

'Then, you think I oughtn't . . .?'

'How can I guess? I'm impressed that you're prepared to try, especially now. But don't be upset if no one believes you, or' – oblique glance – 'if it gets you into yet more trouble.'

'Trouble? I suppose it could. But somebody's got to speak out.'

'As I implied, you're a courageous woman.'

'Courageous? Me?' Eva was astonished. Then another thought struck her. 'I say, though, what about you?'

'What about me?'

'I don't want to make things difficult. . . . I mean, if we go along together. . . .'

She prayed helplessly for that gift of tact which, yet

173

again, had eluded her, for she guessed the image that her words must have evoked. The image of a curtain twitched by an unseen hand. Of a woman, head lowered, whose eyes sought the railing as she walked down the street. How bewildering to contemplate the hold which that drab little woman with her secretive movements, her sly walk, must exercise over him!

He didn't respond. They reached the gates of the new County Hall in silence. There, Eva stopped and turned to face him.

'Well, it might be awkward, mightn't it?'

Had she gone too far? Probably. But she had to give Gerry Smith a chance to extricate himself from the role of knight errant. He said without looking at her: 'You think I'm weak, don't you?'

Eva opened her mouth to expostulate, closed it again. Yes, that was exactly what she thought; but what a wounding thing to put into words. She spoke at last, fumblingly.

'But I don't know your . . . I'm not competent to. . . .'

At least it wasn't a lie, a flat denial. A glance told her he was grateful for that. But it was an evasion. She watched him examine her words.

'Thank you,' he said, polite, depressed.

It burst on her then – good God, the man actually *wanted* imperfect human judgement! Cheeks scarlet, she said abruptly: 'All right, I have thought you weak – and bloody unfriendly, too, if I may say so. I call you Mr Locked-bolted-and-barred. . . .'

She was startled by the relief which lit up his face; but, flushed still, breathless still, she managed to finish: '. . . Today you've shown me I'm wrong. I'm sorry.'

He shook his head, smiling. He said, a bit breathless, too: 'I'd been sent out to buy the onions.'

'What?'

'Onions,' he repeated in a firm voice. 'I'd been told to go and get them. A pound of onions. They were needed, are needed, for lunch. I was to be back by half-past ten.'

'And?'

'And then I saw what was happening at your gate.'

'Oh. So what did you say?'

'I hadn't the courage to say anything.'

'You mean you just came?'

'Yes. Leaving the basket in the porch.'

She thought about it.

'Crikey, you'll catch it, won't you, when you get home?'

'I shall catch it', he echoed, 'when I get home.'

Then suddenly they were laughing; laughing with great gulps of release like adolescents let out of school.

But it was all very well – at least, it was all very well for her, though she could guess what earth-shattering proportions even onions might assume within the context of a grievance; and that he'd done what he'd done for a scandalous neighbour wouldn't help at all.

'But, look . . . I don't want you to . . . I don't want to make things hard. I mean, what on earth can you say?'

'Don't worry about that,' he said, smiling. 'I shall just say I'm free now, that's all.'

'*Just* say you're free?' Eva was awed. 'And *that's all*?'

'It's a fact. I am free now. Not free of Ida, of course – I wouldn't want to be – but free of her tyranny. Though I shall try to be kind about it.'

Eva asked hesitantly: 'How will she . . .?'

'Badly. It's going to be a dreadful shock for poor Ida.'

'Then . . .?'

'Then I shall do my best to understand – and be loving; for I do love her, you know, my wife. She's the woman I chose to marry; that's what I shall think of when her sick headache develops and she gets me up at two o'clock tomorrow morning to make tea which she won't, in the end, drink. Because none of that matters now. It can't touch me. So I may be a bit more use. . . .' He stammered a little. 'What I'd like to do, if it doesn't sound too patronising, is to help her grow up as you', he said to Eva, 'have helped me.'

'I've done nothing! Good heavens, man, it was your gesture, your kindness. . . .'

'It was your courage in the first place. . . .'

'This,' she pointed out, 'is fast turning into a mutual admiration society. I propose we bring the present business to a close.'

He smiled his sweet, wintry smile.

'Seconded. Let's go and see what the Council's spent our money on.'

As they walked up the drive to the entrance he tipped a stone with his toe, then, with a deft kick, sent it soaring. Glancing at him she thought she'd rarely seen a man so simply, straightforwardly happy. His eyes, clear, uncluttered, reflected a state she knew to be joy. Then his face clouded.

'Yes?'

'Had you guessed that Johnson was out of work?'

'Johnson? *Ed?* I most certainly hadn't! Since when?'

'About a year and a half ago – no, rather more.'

'But he goes out – went out – as usual every morning. . . .'

'To keep up appearances. That, and looking for work. He even did a bit of navvying here for a while. . . .'

'*Navvying?* But. . . .'

'I know. Neat suit, furled umbrella, little attaché case. He used to change in the public lavatories. He wasn't ashamed to work with his hands; but he isn't strong, Johnson, and couldn't keep those tough jobs. Above all, he was hurt on Miriam's behalf; felt a failure.'

'Failure? He had excellent qualifications. . . .'

'Which made it all the harder, especially for his wife. They'd had to work their way up, you see. . . . It might not matter to you – perhaps it doesn't – but it matters to Miriam, that kind of thing. She was proud that her husband had a white-collar job.'

'I just can't believe. . . .'

'I assure you it's correct.'

'I don't mean that. I mean I'm ashamed I didn't know. I looked on myself as their friend. Some friend.'

He didn't attempt to comfort her or make things

176

easy; he just looked at her kindly and left her with the thought that she had, perhaps, been as self-centred as she feared.

'How did you find out?' she asked after a moment.

'By chance. I ran into Johnson in the reading room at the library and noticed that he had the *Argus* open at the Jobs Vacant section. One thing led to another and we went out for a couple of beers. That's when he told me.'

'Oh. And he didn't tell me.'

'I wouldn't feel too badly about that. Johnson spoke of you with great warmth. . . .' Gerry Smith hesitated. 'My guess is he didn't want you to know in case you felt responsible.'

'Felt responsible? Me?'

'Johnson seemed to imagine', Smith said awkwardly, 'that the late Councillor Thornby had a hand in easing him out. He implied that there was some link with you, Miss Wootton, but he didn't say what – in fact he asked me not to tell you, which means I'm breaking faith. But, if he's right, I think I should.'

'Yes,' she said, smitten. 'I'm glad you have. Thanks. And Ed?' she asked at last. 'Is he still out of work?'

'I don't know. His house should get a fair price. . . .'

'Except', Eva put in, 'that his house is next to mine.'

'It'd help if you got yours cleaned up, of course.'

'Monday. I'll ring first thing. It just hadn't occurred to me that. . . .'

'I thought you'd want to know.'

'Yes. I still believe it's better to know the truth than be comfortable; but one needs to know it all, and that's not easy.'

'You mean the truth, the whole and nothing but? You're clearly an impossible woman.'

She gave him a tired grin.

'Oh, I am; absolutely impossible!'

He smiled back.

'May I call you Eva?' he asked shyly.

'Of course you may,' she said without hesitation.

Mentally, she put two fingers up to Marty Pike.

22

The new County Hall had been built on comely, wooded land on the outskirts of Tigby. It squatted, a crude, uncompromising block, on a low escarpment over-looking the river – but barely, he murmured, above flood level when February did its worst: there would be problems, no doubt, in the basement.

'Nicer and cleaner the way cats do it,' Eva said morosely. 'At least they bury their dirt.'

For acres around the land had been torn and seamed clumsily together by ruler-drawn roads. It was as though marauding giants had raped the earth and set up this obscene beehive as a place of pilgrimage.

'Someone's tried to adjust the balance, Eva. . . .'

To be fair, someone had. Hundreds of shrubs and trees had been planted and some of them were even still alive. But, recalling the site as she'd first seen it, Eva would not be mollified. There had been beeches then, magnificent mature trees; and, standing as they did in exactly the right place to mask the inevitably unlovely services essential to the running of the County offices, they had been one of the factors in the Council's decision to buy Halley Hall. The mansion, too, had been hailed as an asset, as had the well-maintained stable block which had been earmarked as ideal for the long-promised museum and educational resources centre. The early drawings had been specific on all these points; and she recalled them well, those drawings, as she did the care with which the architect and the Adviser for Horticulture had retained as much as possible of what had so elegantly, in the eighteenth century, been brought into being for gentlemen.

It had all gone. Yet why, and at what a cost, fell those beeches only, at the end of the day and at the wrong time of year, to thrust back immature saplings of lightweight trees which, even if they lived, would be dwarfed into tussocks by the Folly?

'This is the first time you've actually . . .?'

'Yes. I wish now. . . .' She was full of unease. 'The original plans were quite different,' she assured him.

The only plans she'd seen had been those early ones, the great design. When she'd named the place Salwart's Folly it had been on the evidence of rumours and jokes picked up over the past two years. Yet the final drawings must have been through Alec's hands. In no way could they have bypassed him. Yet she, his secretary. . . .

'Some car park, though!' Gerry Smith was saying.

And so it was. Provision for the internal combustion engine was superb. A careful balance of aesthetic and functional considerations – and how many hours had gone on that! – had been set aside to provide an infinity of parking far and away above that estimated need which had so painstakingly been arrived at, so meticulously checked, so grudgingly conceded. A wasteland of asphalt and breeze block obtruded from the very walls of the Folly like some vast indigestible waffle. A shambles. For once Eva agreed with Marty Pike – though not, almost certainly, with his reason for saying it.

'I suppose they knew what they were doing,' Gerry said doubtfully.

'It's called the march of progress – hadn't you heard?'

But those finalised plans which had produced this monstrosity – who had typed the accompanying memo? Or had Alec scribbled it himself before sending the drawings back?

The Folly as a whole might have overtones of megalomaniac meanness, but the main entrance was stately.

179

'Think of the heat loss – just think of it!' Eva mourned.

They had passed through wide and automated doors into a reception hall of noble proportions. Soaring like a cathedral, it seemed to have been constructed of leather, cork and copper with cobbles of startling blue and lemon in place of conventional glazing. So far as Eva could see in the encircling gloom it appeared to be carpeted wall to wall with peacock feathers.

'Lights on all day,' she said, depressed, 'and more lights than this if anyone's to work.'

Out of curiosity she looked for, and found, the control panel. There were sprayed galaxies of light, slow-flooding dawns of light, high noons of radiance, Milton's dim religious light, even a jingle of tarty little coloured lights more befitting a knees-up than serious Council business. This morning, presumably in defer-ence to the energy-crisis lobby – it was, after all, the day of the common ratepayer – only a cleverly selected few had been switched on to illuminate only a few cle-verly selected areas. The overall effect was impressive though obscure. It hinted at an environment – that would be their word, *environment* – where civic dignity could be at home.

'What sods, eh?' she murmured, grinning faintly.

It was a rare acknowledgement of being profession-ally bested. A compliment almost.

A group had already collected in the bay round the empty reception-desk. They seemed diminished by the splendour, ill at ease. One or two were staring with an attempt at sang-froid at the mural – brilliantly lit, that – which had been unveiled when the building was officially opened and about the cost of which as well as its precise meaning – it was called *Democracy* – there was now some question.

She heard a disgusted voice say: 'Modern art, I sup-pose. It has that luke!' and, turning, she found Archie and Moo behind her.

'Well, just look who's . . .!' Embarrassed, Eva

recalled how she'd fled Moo's voice. '. . . Moo, Archie –
how nice!' She glanced at Gerry Smith. 'Do you all
know each other?'

'Ay.' Archie nodded. 'And what do you think to
this?' he asked them.

Together they turned to study the massively painted
wall, part of a Youth Opportunities Scheme project.

'Oh, how *unnecessary*' Moo murmured, averting her
face.

'Never mind about the nude, love. What I want to
know is what's all that stuff like frogspawn?'

Eva twinkled at Gerry. She noticed Moo notice.

'That? I think it's a kind of dreadful truth,
Archie – the Word become trapped bubbles when it
might have been made flesh.'

Archie looked at her, suspicious.

'Oh ay? I suppose if you like modern art. . . . I still
think the lads should've been taught a trade myself.
Plumbing, f'rinstance. Something useful.'

He turned aside to chat to Gerry Smith.

Moo was waiting patiently for Eva. She was a soft
little blob of a woman, like crème Chantilly which had
inadvertently begun to breathe. There was a sugary
gentility in all she said, and she dressed in confection-
ery colours to match.

'It was kind of you to send a welcome home card,'
Eva told her quickly. 'I ought to have thanked you
before.'

'Neighbours . . .' Moo murmured. 'I called out,
only. . . . You know, dear, you should get it rectified.
They can do miracles. *Miracles*. . . .'

'The house? Yes, of course. I'll be on to the company. . . .'

Moo closed her eyes, looked pinkly away. Too late, it
was clear that she had no intention of referring to anything so indelicate as the defacing of the house. Eva
sighed inwardly. She never got it right. The only pre-
dictable element in Moo was her resentment of Doris
Cope.

'Poor Mumsie was a *martyr* to deafness, too,' she was saying, 'in the twilight of her. . . .' She gave Eva a brooding look. 'And did you have a lovely time abroad? I'd be afraid of the drains myself; but, then, I'm hypersensitive. . . .' Her gaze roved back to Gerry. 'How nice that you know Mr Smith so well. It's quite an event, seeing him out with a lady-friend. Now, tell me,' she whispered, turning her full pale eyes on Eva, '*how's Mr Right*?'

'Mr . . .?'

Moo's eyes flickered. 'Don't say you've forgotten him already!'

'Oh, you mean Alec – he's fine.'

'Really?' She peeked distrustfully at Eva. '*We* haven't seen him in a month of Sundays. A real gentleman, Alec,' she conceded. 'Still, he's in local government; he would be. It's a funny thing, dear, but I always felt *very close* to Alec. I shall never forget', she said wistfully, 'that first time we all met. Such a *special* occasion. Archie and I often talk about it.'

'What occasion was that?'

'*Well!*' Moo looked offended. 'The day you moved in, of course. You ought to remember. I passed a dish of trifle over the fence. *Love-birds*, I said to Archie. *I* knew straight off, but he couldn't see it. Alec was planting something. . . . Well, I'm surprised you've forgotten about my trifle, I must say!'

'I hadn't forgotten, Moo; it's just. . . .'

'You never pop in these days, and we were all so *close*. . . . Oh, and I *was so distressed* to read about your poor auntie! What a *tragedy* to pass over while you were away' – Moo breathed it distastefully – '*gadding* . . .! How's *she*, by the way?'

'She?'

Moo shut her eyes again. 'That Periscope woman.'

'Ah, Doris. Busy as usual, yes. She may', Eva added with a touch of malice, 'soon be a neighbour of yours.'

She'd intended no more than that touch of malice, but she felt her spirits lift as she said it. She was going to get out of Tigby! It was as though a breath of sea air had parted the curtains of a sick-room.

'A neighbour of *ours*? How's that?'

'I may sell her my house when I leave.' She put a hand on Gerry's arm. 'Do excuse us now, Moo, will you? I want to see what the Parks Department has done. . . . Goodbye, Archie.'

As they turned away she heard Moo say fretfully: '*She's* going, which is something; but if that Periscope woman. . . .'

'Home, Gerry. I've had enough.'

'What about your questions?'

'No. On mature consideration, as my old chief used to say, I've decided that there must be better ways of putting things right than by being plain damned childish.'

Out of the blue then, like so many things, it came back to her, her childhood concept of God. For years she'd imagined him sitting in a deck chair on Mount Sinai dictating all those Thou-Shalt-Nots while Moses took them down with a hammer and chisel on the back of a few old tombstones. And she'd thought how lucky they were, the Israelites, having it all spelt out for them hot from God's mouth; but at the same time she was sorry for the worshippers of Baal, who, it had seemed to her, were only doing the best they knew.

Which, it still seemed to her, was the trouble with right and wrong; for she longed from the heart to be on the side of the angels in that on-going war in heaven but wasn't always sure which of the choices right was. And how, she asked herself again as they walked to the bus, can one possibly learn a thing like that except by plunging in and sometimes getting it wrong?

23

Dear Doris,

How kind of you to write. Thanks for your commiseration. Yes, I appreciate that the mess and current scandal may well have detracted from the value of my house. . . .

Eva grinned. Neither stupid nor slow off the mark, Doris. She'd keep Moo on her toes all right.

. . . However, I shall be getting things cleaned up as quickly as I can if only for the sake of my good ex-neighbours, the Johnsons, who have just put their house on the market, as you knew may. . . .

Whoops, Freudian slip, Pusscat! Eva changed it to *as you may know.* But of course Doris had known something was in the wind. She realised it now. Why was it that she, Eva, was always the last to tumble to things?

. . . I agree that there's still no reason why we shouldn't come to some arrangement which suits ourselves – prior to the essential legalities, naturally. I'm all for cutting out the man. . . .

Freud again. She inserted *middle* before *man.*

. . . But I'm afraid I can't give you a precise date. . . .

A precise date. She'd been waiting for a precise date for nearly ten and a half years, and here was Doris expecting to have one by return of post! And yet why not? Suppose she gave Alec a month – for there was always that nagging possibility, the hospital bed: but she'd never known him sulk for longer than a fortnight, so in four weeks. . . .

The main thing was to get out of Tigby. Of that she

was now sure in the same way as she was sure about going to Harriets. Answering Doris's note, which she'd found pushed through her door when she got back from her visit to the Folly that morning, was helping her to think out the tactics of the move; but how glad she was that she'd made up her mind about the move itself before getting that note.

Oh, if only Alec would ring! But the words came mechanically to her now as did the calculation – Saturday today, Sunday tomorrow; perhaps in Monday morning's post, less than two days. . . . Still, if there was more waiting to be endured, then there were places other than Tigby to wait in. Psychically, she had left Tigby behind her already. She felt like Pilgrim when the burden rolled from his back.

. . . *Can't give you a precise date, though I would expect to let you have possession in something like four weeks. . . .*

Eva's spirits lifted with every line. To make things happen; to have them in one's hands rather than be at their mercy, that was important, like having a structure for the day.

. . . *So pop in*, she encouraged Doris. Pop. *and the sooner the better. I'm sure you'll want to assess the place thoroughly before making me an offer – I leave it to you to arrange for a survey – and I, of course,* she added, grinning – for why be a sucker all the time, Pussy? – *will need to take advice on the figure you suggest before I decide.*

I hope you enjoyed the weekend weaving course. Ever, Eva.

She addressed and stamped an envelope. That sorted Doris out.

Eva rarely went into the spare bedroom; but she found herself there now, looking down on the garden. The wych-elm might be dead but everything else was boisterously, thrustingly alive; and at the heart of that resurrection, buried under the plum tree in the middle of the grass, lay Pussy. Eva smiled, suddenly touched to see to what green use those inadequate remains had been put.

But how brightly it stood out still against the dead adjacent bark of the wych-elm, that Christmas tree of theirs. Eva studied the two trees, troubled. If time had run out for the wych-elm, then the wych-elm would have to go. She'd arrange for its despatch when she arranged for her house to be cleaned. Why had it taken her so long to accept the fact that the wych-elm was dead? It hadn't put out leaves last spring, or the spring before. When, in fact, how long ago, had she seen the wych-elm in healthy leaf?

She could no longer remember. Only that she'd wanted life to be there, had clung to the belief that life was there, that there must be life – latent, perhaps, but life; and she'd willed it to flourish, that life which she'd believed must be waiting only for a luckier spring.

Well.

Eva glanced at her watch. Nearly time to leave for her interview at Harriets; and she grinned – as Idris would not have done – as she thought about that non-job which, it seemed, she was instructed to seek. Odd that her decision to leave Tigby made no difference – against reason, that. Yet there she was, certain that her feet were on the road she should travel by, and she contemplated it, serene.

But poor Idris! How bitter to discover that his prize pupil was a woman first, an intelligence second.

Back in her own bedroom she picked up the lump of driftwood, which – but when? – she must have put down by the phone.

And Alec?

It came to her then without surprise that Alec was in the past. In a moment of inattention the link between them had gone. There was a gap now where something living had once been, and she must accept it. What, in any case, could one do with actuality but accept it? That letter of hers might just as well have been posted from the cliff's edge, launched into a high wind. It was no more than a thing to be taken by the tide and lost at sea.

Eva felt no pain yet, only knowledge. Perhaps pain, too, like growth, would be a matter of time.

Ten more minutes. She straightened her brush and comb and, without looking at it, took down the bon voyage card and dropped it in the bin. Something white, obtruding from the drawer in the bedside table, caught her eye, and she pulled out the whole drawer, tipping its contents on to the counterpane. Such a mess, such a muddle. How can one live like this! she scolded.

Eva smoothed out the crumpled photograph of the gang – Gwen, Mario, Latchy, a beaming stranger who was herself. . . .

Latchy? That she had even had thoughts that Latchy might be the magic which would transform her life! That, by repeating the blind pattern of dependence, she would be saved the trouble of working out the equation for herself!

She sighed as she shook her head at the child within; then she began to sort out the oddments from the drawer – curlers, an old lipstick, receipted bills, safety-pins. . . .

She came on it last of all, a yellowing print, and turned it, curious. A voice spoke to her from the back of her head: a right Tigbeian, that one!

She found she was gazing into Alec's face.

It was a press photograph, a reject – she'd forgotten she had it – taken at the office ball their first year in Tigby. Alec, by mischance, had stepped into the range of a camera which was seeking someone else; and smiling, deprecating, too late, had tried to dissociate himself.

'Alec. . . .'

His bald patch had been the merest hint of a tonsure in those days but, that apart, Eva could see little change. His eyes were set in their expression of candid benevolence which she so loved, so distrusted, and there seemed to be the hesitant beginnings of a denial on those parted lips. About his whole person there was an air of having been caught at a moment when he was poised for flight.

'Is it true, then?' she asked him sadly.

She examined them with love, that golden smile, the wide and trusting eyes which revealed so little, hid so much; then she tore the photograph across and threw the pieces into the bin.

24

There was no one at reception. Eva pressed the bell on the desk as she glanced about her. No flowers – what a pity; and the whole place dingier than she remembered it.

She'd been to Harriets only once before, to that office ball where the photograph of Alec had been taken. She'd gone reluctantly, and her forebodings had been right; she'd had a wretched evening. One by one her colleagues had dutifully asked her to dance; but, recently arrived, she scarcely knew them and each, in any case, had brought a partner. But, yes, they'd done what they could, while she, over the shoulder of one semi-stranger after another, had watched Alec.

She'd told him beforehand that he was neither to ask her to dance nor to let Jean know she was there, so she could hardly complain. Nevertheless, it didn't help to see him dancing with Jean; especially as he made a point of smiling at her over Jean's head and – or so it seemed to her – of holding Jean that little bit closer as he smiled.

She'd never been to a staff ball since – and what a deprivation that was; a decade without dancing, she who so loved to dance.

Eva rang the bell a second time and, after a moment, the door beyond the desk opened and a woman hurried through.

'Good evening, madam.'

One sweep of those professionally smiling eyes took in the fact that Eva had no suitcase. Another assessed her person. The brows went up.

'I rang yesterday – Eva Wootton. About the job.'

'Oh.'

'I was given an appointment – though I realise, of course, that the post may have been filled since. . . .'

'Well, not actually. . . . I mean I don't think anything's been finalised yet.'

There was a pause.

'I've brought my certificates,' Eva said briskly, 'and a testimonial from my last employer – I worked for the County Council. If you need confidential references, I can. . . .'

'That'll be Johnnie's department,' the woman said quickly. 'You'd better give them to him.'

'Johnnie?'

'Mr Banbury – he sees to staff and so on.'

The woman was embarrassed. Something was wrong; in fact the whole atmosphere was wrong. And where was she supposed to find him, this Mr Banbury? Eva smiled back at the woman with a confidence she no longer felt. Yet she'd been so sure she should come, so certain. . . .

There was a harsh sound of tyres on gravel as a car drew up. Then a door slammed. The woman brightened.

'Ah, here she is! We're expecting an overnight guest,' she explained. 'Trust him, when I'm supposed to be off duty! But that's life – it is here, any road! Now, Miss Wootton – it is *Miss* Wootton, isn't it? – why don't you wait in the snug and I'll get Mr Banbury down to see you just as soon as I can – right? This way, dear.'

As Eva followed she was aware of the front door opening behind her.

'Be with you in two ticks, madam! Here it is,' she told Eva. 'Make yourself at home.'

And she shut her in with a gridded bar counter, some glossy magazines and an odour of stale smoke. That, and a sense of unreality.

Eva looked cautiously about her. Cheap paper, thinned-out paint, a fine Chinese rug which needed cleaning. . . . Without conscious effort she'd made a list of the room's defects and the action which should be taken to rectify them. It was as though, once again, she'd gone out with Alec, clipboard in hand, alert, concerned, zealous to safeguard the interests of the people she served. Like a wound-up toy, her working self had twitched into motion; had begun to process this alien data, assume a new loyalty. She regarded herself with astonishment. How could it have any part in her now, this efficient mechanical doll which still seemed to share her skin? It had no connection with her real concerns. All that was past.

So, sitting on the too-low sofa trying to keep her back straight and her plump little legs decorously together, Eva emptied her mind and, serene again, waited.

She was suddenly aware that she was no longer alone. A young man stood framed in the doorway looking down on her, the receptionist at his shoulder.

Eva struggled up out of the soggy cushions – though could he really be the manager, a youngster like that?

'Mr Banbury . . .?'

The man looked her over without replying. She watched his eyes go from the tightly-stretched cloth across her belly to the little bulges of fat below her bra, and from there to the line of her jaw and – yes, she could have sworn it – to the tiny pink disc over which she had so carefully fluffed her hair.

Out of habit – habit again – she proffered a bright smile.

He said to the receptionist, unsmiling: 'Why do you always have to waste my time?'

'If I tell you, I'm wrong. If I don't tell you, I'm still wrong.' The woman was unsmiling too. 'So, all right, I'm wrong. Have it your own way.'

'You could try using your common sense.'

'It was you drafted the ad,' she reminded him, sharp. 'What did you expect?'

'I said "mature"; I didn't say "geriatric". This is a

191

country club not an old folks' home. Get rid of her,' he told the receptionist as he went.

The woman flushed.

'It's all right, really it is!' Eva assured her.

For it was all right. She was speaking the truth. She felt nothing; nothing at all except pity for the woman.

'Don't take no notice. Don't let him upset you. Ignorant?' the receptionist said bitterly. 'I've had my bibful with that jumped-up little tramp! Moods? Real cheap he can be, like tonight; yet if you'd come yesterday or some other time when his lordship was feeling a bit more agreeable he'd not only have given you the job he'd have asked you to dinner as well.'

'Honestly, it doesn't matter.'

'Still, you're better out of it, if that's any comfort – and I ought to know, I'm married to him! All right, then, a drink before you. . . . No, Miss Wootton, I insist; it's the very least. . . . That, and your taxi fares, of course. . . .' She busied herself with locks, rolled the grid aside. 'Been here before, dear?'

'Yes, I. . . .'

'Isn't that nice? That's a comfier chair, by the way, the one opposite the window. And take my tip and have the brandy. There's nothing like brandy for making a woman feel she is a woman, if you know what I mean.' She poured two generous measures, handed one to Eva. 'Well, dear, the skin orf it, as the rabbi said to the. . . .' The door opened and Mrs Banbury put down her glass. 'You found everything you wanted, madam?'

'Yes, thank you.'

It was a woman's voice, pleasing; not a voice she'd have associated with Harriets at all.

'I'm off this evening; but give Mr Banbury a tinkle if. . . . Your usual?'

'Please.'

'Plenty of ice, isn't it?'

'Yes, plenty of ice and topped right up with soda.'

Not a voice she'd have associated with Harriets but a voice which, dimly, she felt she knew. Eva turned.

'Hel-*lo*! It *is* Eva Wootton? It must be! Eva Wootton at last!' And, dumb, Eva found herself face to face with Jean.

'Oh. I. . . .'

She broke off, looked helplessly at Alec's wife.

Without waiting for an invitation Jean sat down by her.

'You've found a friend? That's nice,' Mrs Banbury said. 'Just help yourself to what you want, Mrs Burroughs, and chalk it up.' She looked at each in turn. 'Dinner?'

Jean tilted her head questioningly.

'No, thank you,' Eva said quickly.

'Won't you? It'd be company for. . . .'

'Really. But thank you all the same.'

'Just one, then? Usual table, usual time. . . . And don't forget', she said in a lowered voice to Eva, 'to pick up that envelope at the office. I'll have it ready. Better luck next time, eh? And how's Mr Burroughs these days?' she asked Jean.

'His usual self.'

'That's nice. Mind you give him my . . .' The telephone in the hall rang. 'Now, what the asterisk's that!'

The door closed on Mrs Banbury. There was a moment of constraint. Eva heard herself swallow.

'Well,' Jean said. She put her drink on the table, opened her bag and paused, hand half-inside. 'Oh, damn! I keep forgetting I've given the filthy habit up!' The bag shut with a snap. 'And I don't even carry worry beads!' Their eyes met, and Jean smiled at her. 'Isn't life hell?'

Eva said simply: 'Yes. I talk to the cat.'

'Well, what's wrong with talking to the cat? Better than worry beads or fags or the drink. At least a cat's got feelings.'

'Not this cat. I talk to a dead cat.' Suddenly at ease, Eva grinned back. 'And we weren't even lovely and pleasant in our lives. He smelt horrible, Pussy.'

She looked frankly at Jean for the first time, let her

eyes examine Jean's face; and those eyes which had smiled up at Alec, teasing, that long-ago Sunday were on her, accepting, friendly.

But how Jean had aged! And was Jean perhaps thinking the same about her, and that she was too old now for lovers?

'Well, come on, I want to hear all about that retirement of yours!' Jean invited. 'You left when?'

'A month ago yesterday.'

'And?'

'Took a tour – three weeks of it: Greece, the islands, Italy. . . . One of those package jobs. Everything laid on.'

'And it was bliss?' Jean asked, polite.

'No, it wasn't bliss. It was one long boozy dazzle of beaches and chumminess with the odd ruin thrown in. I ate too much, drank too much, spent too much. . . . It was one of the silliest things I ever did in my life. But I reckon I'd do it again.' She could see Jean probing her words. 'Make a gesture, I mean. Two fingers.'

Jean's face lit up.

'I know! I know *exactly* . . .!'

They approved each other, the women, nodding.

'So you made your gesture – good! And now you're back and, I hope,' Alec's wife – Alec's ex-wife – encouraged her, 'enjoying what they call being a lady of leisure?'

Eva threw her an oblique smile.

'At the moment I miss my chains – isn't that an awful thing to have to admit? And until I find something to put in their place. . . .'

What a relief, though, actually to admit it! Alec had been right – at least, he'd been right about this: she and Jean would have got on well together.

'Yes. One needs a framework.'

'That's it – a framework.'

Eva glanced at her. Jean's eyes were fixed on a fine group of horse-chestnut trees which stood, flushed with evening light, just beyond the window; and as she studied that half-averted face she recalled that Jean, too, had lost her framework, had, presumably, tossed it away out of accumulated rage and hurt as she herself had done. And how deep was it, she wondered uneasily, that hurt for which she, with Alec, was responsible?

'So what next, Eva?'

'I'm not sure yet; except that I'm leaving Tigby.'

'But didn't I gather, from what Mrs Banbury hissed . . .?'

'That I came here for a job and didn't get it? Yes.' Eva grinned at her. 'At the moment I'm in the throes of being got rid of.'

'Got rid of?'

'Because I'm old, you see,' Eva said without rancour, 'because I've got fat. It wouldn't do' – she grinned again – 'for the gentlemen.'

'Did you want the job?'

'Good God, no!'

'And you're leaving Tigby?'

'Yes.'

'Then, why – if you don't mind my asking . . .?'

Eva hesitated. She swirled the brandy round its balloon of glass, watching the oily flow.

'To be truthful,' she said at last, 'and I'd like to be truthful with you, I was somehow prodded into coming here tonight. I don't know how else to say it. So here I am. And here you are.' She raised her eyes to Jean. 'I think', she said carefully, 'it might have been to meet you, to lay ghosts.'

Jean's glass knocked against the edge of the table as she put it down. In the silence they heard curtains drawn in a distant room, then somebody switched on a television set.

Eva looked up to find Jean watching her.

'Are you sure you won't eat with me?'

'It's very kind of you, Mrs Burroughs, but. . . .'

She jumped when Alec's wife shouted: '*Jean*, for God's sake! At least do that for me!'

195

'I'm sorry' – startled – 'Jean.'

'That's better.'

They smiled, but warily now; measured each other. Someone shut that distant door, and the house was silent again.

'I do like you, you know, Eva,' Jean said suddenly. 'I actually *like* you, damn your eyes! Right from the start I knew I'd like you, only I'd have preferred you to be my best friend, not his.'

'Oh. . . .'

Caught off guard, Eva blushed. Jean laughed outright.

'And you never once came to tea!' she mocked. 'Shame!'

'But . . .,' Eva began, confused, 'if you'd already guessed – because I assume from what you've just said that you did, in fact, realise early on that I – that I had, was. . . .'

'That you were sleeping with my husband? Yes, I knew.'

'Then why did you go on ringing me up?'

Jean gave her a curious look. 'Why did I . . .?'

'If you knew I was Alec's mistress, why did you invite me to your house?'

'What are you implying? That you thought I didn't know?'

'Of course. He told me you hadn't guessed, and. . . . Oh, I felt dreadful!' Her cheeks burnt, but it had to be said. 'I mean, look, how could I possibly face you when you didn't know that – I'm sorry, Jean – that I was expecting to marry Alec myself.'

'So you were expecting to marry Alec?'

'Yes. I'm sorry.'

Pink as strawberry lollies, the white flowers of the horse-chestnuts glowed in her gaze. Jean said abruptly: 'You've heard we're divorced?'

'Last Tuesday. The doorman at County Hall told me.'

'The. . . . You mean Alec didn't write?'

'I haven't heard from. . . . Not a proper letter. . . . Not. . . .'

Jean's hand was out. She passed her the empty glass. 'Rémy Martin?'

'Oh, whatever they've got, thanks. . . .'

The great silence of the house hung about them, a backcloth for every tiny sound – the rustle of Jean's dress, the impact of their refilled glasses on the table top, the faint squeak of the leather cushion as Jean sat down again.

'And how is Alec?' Eva asked, awkward. 'Or don't you . . .?'

Jean picked up her glass. She raised it to Eva before drinking, then put the glass carefully back, aligning the bottom with the damp ring on the table.

'Married.'

'I beg your . . .?'

'I should have said remarried.'

'*Married?* A . . .?' Eva's throat closed on the name. 'When was that?' she said at last.

'This afternoon. Which is why. . . . Oh, to hell with it!' Jean tore open her handbag, extricated cigarettes and a lighter. 'There! Six weeks' abstinence down the drain – and two fingers to that as well!' She lit up greedily. 'Sorry, will you . . .?'

Eva shook her averted head. Jean studied it with raised brows, drew deeply on the smoke, let it drift from her nostrils.

'You think he's worth your tears?'

'I'm blowing my nose.'

There was a clash of voices in the hall – Mr and Mrs Banbury having words. The front door slammed.

'Who is she?'

Eva hadn't meant to ask. If Alec had indeed married again, what did it matter who she was, this woman he'd chosen. Except that she had to know.

Jean hesitated. 'His secretary.'

Eva tried to smile. Suddenly, she was desperately tired. She could have fallen asleep where she sat.

'It seems to have become a habit.'

'I wouldn't say so. This one's base metal to her rotten

197

little core. But she's young and she's got the figure of a gazelle – wouldn't it make you spit!'

So she needn't, after all, have asked. She knew, had guessed since time began, had always known the truth she feared.

'So he married Lorraine Hampstead.'

'I wasn't going to tell you that.'

'Then Angela lied.'

'Angela?'

'No, perhaps she didn't lie. . . . It's not important.'

But back her mind went to it then, her first thought, the thing which was important. Adolescent children in Lorraine's care? Were they? That would be intolerable. She glanced at Jean, at her already-empty glass; and, catching her eye, Jean said, aggressive: 'Oh, drink up! Or sing a comic song or something!' She lit a second cigarette, but after a couple of puffs ground it into the ashtray, breaking it across like a stuffed leg. She got up and helped herself to more brandy. 'But don't try to tell me you didn't realise what was going on in that damned love nest of an office!' She held out her hand for Eva's glass. 'Another?'

'No, thanks.'

Jean slumped down, drank again.

'Of course you knew! That was half the fun for him; he'd have rubbed your nose in it!' She fumbled with her cigarettes, looked at Eva over them, hand poised. 'What a victim you were, Eva Wootton – what a fucking feeble victim! Why did you let the bastard get away with everything? That's what made me so mad!'

'You didn't exactly challenge him yourself,' Eva said mildly.

'Meaning what by that remark?'

'That he got away with plenty with you.'

'Got away with . . .? *Him?* He got away with nothing!' Jean boasted. 'It was you were the softy!'

'He got away with me!' Eva said, stung.

Jean gazed at her, blinked a little.

'Oh, come off it!' Her lips curved in a slow smile. 'You can't seriously believe that.'

'Why not? It's true, isn't it?'

'It is not true,' Jean purred, feline, claws just showing.

'What do you mean, not true? All right, you may have *guessed*. . . . But did you ever challenge? Or was that why you asked me to the house? Did you plan to have a showdown there, play it out on your own home ground . . .? In which case,' Eva cried, flustered now, for Jean was still smiling, 'in *which* case . . .!'

'But there was no need for a showdown. If I knew about you – as I did from the very first night, and make no mistake about that – it wasn't because I'd guessed but because Alec told me. Don't look at me like that, Eva; it's true. He could hardly wait for me to get home so that he could spill it out. He was tickled pink – yet another scalp, and the one he'd least expected, the bluestocking. Lucky old Alec!'

'*Alec* told you?'

'Alec told me. We were' – sardonically – 'husband and wife, remember.'

'He discussed me with you? It was Alec . . .?'

'We had a house rule – so long as I knew, no recriminations. But God help him if he had something on the side and didn't tell me.'

'I don't believe you!' Eva cried, shocked.

'Then, it's very silly of you. You should.'

'But Alec wouldn't do an awful thing like that!'

Jean's smile left her. She considered Eva for a long moment in silence.

'Wouldn't he? Not even if it suited him?' Eva dropped her eyes. 'Yes, you fell for it, didn't you? You're soft,' Jean said with affectionate exasperation, 'you're the original marshmallow! Did nobody ever teach you how to take care of yourself?'

After a while Eva said: 'I still don't understand.'

'What don't you understand, Marshmallow?'

'Why you invited me to your house, knowing. . . .'

'Oh, that.'

'Yes. I'd like to know.' And when Jean didn't respond: 'I feel I must know, if you don't mind.'

Jean spread her fingers, examined her rings.

'Very well. I invited you because Alec pressed me to.' She glanced at Eva. 'So there you are.'

'Alec . . .?'

'Yes.'

'Are you saying that you and Alec connived . . .?'

'Yes. He . . . I. . . .'

'Go on.'

'You've got to realise that Alec had a need to involve me with . . . with. . . . Look, Eva, when you gave him an Easter egg he fed me bits of it in bed – right? While we were making love. Telling me . . . talking about. . . .' She shot a look at Eva's uncomprehending gaze. 'Oh, for God's sake, do I have to spell it out!' she cried, tears coming at last. 'Some marriages need an Eva, and ours was one. But it was a marriage. In a lot of ways it was a very good marriage; and I was determined', she went on, dabbing at her eyes, 'that I was going to keep it intact.'

'I see,' Eva said, mystified.

Jean almost howled at her: 'But you don't see – you're too decent! This is right out of your league!'

The shadows were long now, fingering their way east across the lawn, the sky pale and infinitely remote.

'That's the missing bit of the jigsaw,' Eva said at last.

'Jigsaw?'

'I spied on you once, Jean. . . .'

And, hesitantly, she told Alec's ex-wife about the little love scene she'd watched being played out in the garden; about how she'd known then that they were a real couple but wouldn't face it.

Jean's tears welled again.

'A real couple? Yes, we were. Even though we may have talked about what you were like in bed – you, or Karen before you, or Helena before Karen . . .'

'And later Lorraine Hampstead?'

'And later Lorraine bloody Hampstead – the only one of his women I actually hated, and that's the one he had to marry!'

Eva tried to thrust it from her again, but this time pain forced it out.

'Which of you has custody of the children?' It jerked from her, an accusation almost. 'Though they must be big now,' she offered quickly, trying to make amends. 'Almost independent.'

'What children are these?' Jean asked, bending to pick up her lighter.

'Why, Alec's, yours. . . .'

'And how many' – straightening up – 'are we supposed to have?'

'Just the boy and the . . .' Eva frowned at her. '*Supposed* to have?'

'Did you ever see a photograph of our wee mites?'

'Well, no,' Eva said uncertainly. 'Alec didn't show me one, so I assumed it was because he didn't want to hurt. . . .'

'Oh, Marshmallow, Marshmallow!' Jean tried to smile at her. 'With Alec in the home, do you imagine there'd be room for yet another child?' For the second time that evening, but gently now, she said: 'Don't look at me like that.'

After a while Eva nodded. 'That explains it. I thought the garden looked too tidy.'

'Garden?'

'That day I told you about. It was the children I'd really come to see, to have a picture in my mind, to make up for. . . . Because that's why Alec wouldn't leave you – wouldn't leave you for me, I mean; that's what he said. Not until the children had grown. . . .' She smiled faintly at Jean. 'And there were no toys there, not one. It seemed so strange – I expected a swing. . . .' She thought about it, smiled again. 'I'd have taken him from you if I could, you know; but the thought of hurting those children. . . . And now you tell

201

me there are no children, never were children.'

Jean was on her feet. She swept up their glasses.

'Just a little one. . . . Sorry.'

Eva turned to watch her at the bar.

'All those years when I dreaded meeting you. . . .'

'You mean *Wife Bites Secretary: Romance Suspected*?'

'Something like that.'

Jean said cautiously: 'Eva. . . .'

'Yes?'

'You weren't just one of those women, you know. If I implied you were – well, I can be jealous, too; and I had cause; I was. But you were very special to Alec.'

'Oh, no, please! Don't you lie to me as well!'

'It isn't a lie,' Jean said soberly. 'Just something I don't much care to admit. Oh, but come on, Eva; you must have known it. I did, and I could have strangled you!' She glanced up. 'Do you know what I did once? I gave you to Alec as a Christmas present!'

Stabbed, Eva shut her eyes.

'Ah, you don't like that, do you?' Jean said, watching her. 'But it's a fact – as you were a fact, and a fact I had to come to terms with. Because our marriage may have needed you, Marshmallow; but, by God, I didn't! Not as a woman I didn't!'

'No. I can see that. I'm sorry.' There was a pause. 'Tell me about. . . .'

'Oh, that. It was nothing, really. . . .'

'Please tell me.'

'All right, then. It was that first Christmas. He'd got the Tigby job, but we hadn't moved; and one way and another I'd had about all I could take – the devious deal with Tigby, a house I'd been left to dispose of and, final straw' – she made a face at Eva – 'the woman Wootton leaving in hot pursuit. So I walked out on him. I went off on my own to Paris. Alec came back to Garchester expecting the usual Yuletide cheer and found nothing but an empty house and a note on the Christmas tree: *You can have Eva Wootton for*

Christmas, and the best of British! Or something to that effect – all very vulgar, like the dreadful tree.' Jean giggled sadly. 'And I went to such lengths! Tinsel, ghastly little glass things, a gruesome doll. . . . I pinned the note to the doll's skirt. Childish,' she apologised, 'but even then I realised you were a serious contender, that I'd have to keep my wits about me, slap him down now and then. Which, really, is what I'm trying to say; that you were special. I wouldn't have dreamt of walking out on him for anyone else.'

The soft deep note of the dinner gong grew on the silence, became urgent, died away – like the act of love, Eva thought. Perhaps Jean shared the thought, for she raised her head and they smiled briefly at each other – neither, now, capable of speech, both too proud to cry.

Eva flexed the fingers which wavered in her vision, absently assessing their span. She turned her hand and cupped it, remembering the sand which had run through those fingers like water, like silk, spooling back to be lost above the driftline on that faraway Sunday seashore.

25

Dry-eyed, Eva stood alone in the women's room. White tiles and basins, ubiquitous mirrors, a pitiless light. Seven cubicle doors discreetly shut. An attendant's chair on a dais, high-backed, leather-seated, authoritative.

It could have been some hygienic confessional, or a courthouse where judgement and cleansing went hand in hand.

Alec. Was this, then, Alec?

Like a disregarded detail brought into sudden sharp focus by the camera's selective eye, like a familiar image strangely inverted in bright water, she had been shown Alec as another woman saw him. As his ex-wife saw him.

This was Alec as, until now, she would have denied him to be, even to herself. This was Alec as, in that submerged and wiser part of herself, she'd always known he was.

Eva turned on the cold tap and bathed her eyes. Head bowed, she held the sodden handkerchief to the back of her neck until all its coolness had gone.

And now Alec was married to Lorraine Hampstead. Had Lorraine, then, sent that bon voyage card? Probably. What was certain was that she'd followed Alec to the new job. They must have set it up together under her nose before he left Tigby – as he and she had set it up in Garchester under Karen's nose, though she hadn't, until now, appreciated the fact that was Karen.

No need to ask any more who'd typed the memo

agreeing the Folly's final plans. No need to wonder at his last-minute decision to attend its opening: Lorraine had told him she was safely away.

So there it was: another pattern, the same pieces. Everything had changed, nothing was changed; it just depended where one stood.

And she, Eva, had chosen. . . .

Chosen – that was the point. She'd chosen to dismiss as fantasy the actuality of Lorraine while choosing to accept as reality the fantasy of Alec's children. Yet these were key decisions, the fixed points by which she'd charted her conscious course. And both were wrong. Each time two ways had been open to her; each time she'd made her choice against the promptings of that stifled inner self. Nothing was new about any of this; it was just that she'd chosen not to know about it before.

Eva wrung out the handkerchief, put it, chill, against her feverish cheeks. Had she, then, so great a need to be deceived? Was it real, that fear of seeing Alec as he was? But, if she'd refused to see and accept him as he was, how could she have loved him as she ought, this man she'd chosen to love, this man who'd now chosen to marry Lorraine Hampstead?

Could need feel like love? Was the concept of choice yet another illusion? Was her need so great that she wasn't free to choose? If the dance is for puppets, how can the puppets know?

The cloakroom door opened and two women came in. They entered talking animatedly, but when they saw Eva they fell silent. The first opened the nearest lavatory cubicle; the other, head averted, passed her and made for the last.

Eva went on bathing her face. Clearly, she wasn't their concern.

In quick succession, two cisterns flushed. The women emerged simultaneously, aligned themselves at adjacent washbasins. They rinsed their hands, touched up their faces, fingered their hair.

'Have you a little gilt safety-pin?' one asked the other.

'I always carry them with me, dear, gilt safety-pins.'

Islanded by their exclusion, Eva barely noticed them go.

And herself – what of her? How credible was this witness?

Credible? Stifling the truth she affected to seek, ambivalent, of impaired judgement, dependent, pitiful – was that how Eva Wootton stood in the eyes of God? It was easier to accept Alec as he was than to accept this; as it was easier to pray, *forgive us our trespasses as we* . . . than *forgive them their trespasses as I forgive myself who trespass against them.*

Or it was if one was Eva Wootton.

For it was all very well, but Alec hadn't been alone in duplicity nor Jean in connivance. Were her own hands so clean?

'Well?' Eva asked, arrested under that all-revealing light, surrounded by mirrors which, should she choose to look, could show her herself as she was.

Then suddenly, without calculation, she stopped fighting, allowed that the conflict was done. Weary, with nothing left to nerve herself to strive for, Eva gave up; and judgement stood in her like a core of crystal. Emotion in suspense – emotion was irrelevant – she surveyed her botched life; the evasions, dishonesties; opportunities missed, the wrong roads taken and so many broken ends. And what a pity, she thought, how sad it all is; for she had glimpsed the grand design that should have been Eva Wootton and seen it reduced to a folly, and by herself.

She didn't try to justify what she'd become – how could one justify a thing like that? – but, standing under the unshadowed light, she accepted that it was so, that she was thus; and in that moment she knew above all deserving and beyond all doubt that justification had, once and for all time, been freely given.

Her heart bounded, and 'Yes!' she whispered, 'Yes!'

For with all her faults and inadequacies Eva could not but say yes to life, and it was life that had just been offered her.

Like the albatross, her guilt fell away; and, dissolved in grace, she dared at last to weep: not for the gross errors – they had been dealt with, their time was past – but from the depths of her vulnerability she wept for Jean's Christmas tree, which Alec had planted in her garden, for the fairy doll top-heavy with anger and hurt, for tinsel which glittered under the enthusiastic stars but revealed itself as tawdry when morning came, for mud disregarded on their shoes and, yes, for Alec's eyes which had lifted to look at her with imperfect human love across his dishonoured gift.

After a while, calm now, she bathed her cheeks again. Then, as she straightened up, a face – unsought, unprepared for – flashed back at her from the mirror over the basin.

Nora's relative!

Eva stared incredulously into her own startled eyes. Now she'd made the connection she saw that the likeness was uncanny. So that's who Sean Feenan had reminded her of – herself. He could have been her brother, her twin.

26

He was her brother, her twin.

Stunned, Eva fingered the sheets of mauve note-paper, the scent of violets long since gone. She glanced again at the first page. The letter was dated a decade before and enclosed with it was a faded snapshot. Her father – their father, rather, hers and Sean's. A young man in a straw hat.

So she wasn't nobody's child! The knowledge overwhelmed her. She had an identifiable family, a history, roots. She even knew the names under which they had been registered – Sean Edward and Evangeline Hogan, Nora's children.

Eva had woken up to the pealing bells of All Saints, at peace with herself. As she dressed she switched on the news and found that Tigby had hit the headlines. Since dawn, it seemed, delegations from all over England had been streaming into the town to demonstrate against the Blackshirt rally which was to take place that afternoon. Police leave had been cancelled and extra men drafted in. The Home Secretary, caught off guard on his way to early service with his wife, was trapped into saying that he thought the Council's decision to allow such a meeting highly regrettable.

Then Marty Pike came briefly on the air to defend that decision. No, he could not agree. Indeed, he professed himself astonished that the Home Secretary – who was, it grieved him to say, a member of the party he supported – had abused his high office by making what could only be construed as a direct attack by the central arm on the democratic processes of local government. No doubt the Home Secretary had his reasons, but. . . .

'You twisty sod!' Eva admired, settling down to listen.

Again, no; he must be allowed to correct that impression. This was a private meeting – he would stress, *private* – and the elected members of Tigby had been given adequate assurances that it would be conducted in a disciplined manner. Yes, he was satisfied with the arrangements for transport and traffic control. Yes, the police as always. . . .

The smooth voice got a word in at last.

'But is it not true, Councillor, that this rally has been organised by an extremist – I might say militant – fascist group which is known. . . .'

'Why must you media men always stick labels on people? This rally has been organised by Englishmen, ratepayers, citizens of Tigby. They have as much right to their opinions as you or me.'

'But wouldn't you concede that a fascist rally will give offence to many thousands who lost their loved ones in the thirty-nine to forty-five war against. . . .'

'The thirty-nine forty-five war was fought to protect fundamental democratic principles, of which the right to peaceful assembly is one.'

'You stand by that, Councillor Pike?'

'I stand by that.' Marty Pike's voice shook with emotion as, indeed, befitted a Tigbeian who, at last, was addressing the nation. 'It is a sacred trust.'

'Thank you, Councillor Pike. The present spell of good weather is likely to continue for a few more. . . .'

'Fundamental democratic pussycat!' Eva snorted, switching off. Tigby? Thank God she was leaving. But to go where? Do what? That needed some thought.

Then halfway down the stairs she paused. There was an envelope on the mat. Eva sighed. It couldn't be Mrs Breem saying that as a respectable widow she wouldn't do Eva's cleaning any more; nor Moo, with an oblique reference to trifle, begging her not to sell to Doris: those notes had been waiting for her last night. Perhaps Bob's old lady was making doubly sure she wasn't expecting cake. Well, if it was yet more dirty anonymous mail it was yet more dirty anonymous mail and that's all there was to it. She found herself walking more cautiously, though, ready to ward it off, whatever it might be that had come to smite her peace.

But it wasn't anonymous mail. It was a mauve envelope to which was stapled a bus office compliments slip bearing her address. Beyond all hope, Nora had got in touch.

She read it again, read slowly, still shattered, still savouring her joy.

My Dear Daughter,

I have written the word at last who often longed to speak it if only to bring you to your senses. . . .

It was Nora's voice, her mother's voice; unmistakably hers.

. . . But I shall be dead when you get this and so released from my promise to Aileen and you can learn what I was wishful for you to know from the start, for I am not ashamed that it is myself and Ned Feenan you are sprung from. You also have a twin brother, Sean being by half an hour the elder and brought up by Ned's people in their name. Now don't from this be lepping to the conclusion that you are not a bastard after all because you are. . . .

Eva shouted with joy as she read it. Bastard? She'd never felt less like a bastard in her life.

Cracked and yellowed with time, the print lay like a dead leaf on her palm. So this was the lad who had so fecklessly fathered her. Jaunty, chin high, boater rakishly tipped, he grinned up, unrepentant; and Eva shook her head at him, laughing, weeping. For this was her grin, her own defiant stance. It could have been Eva Wootton at twenty telling fate to get stuffed.

A father, a mother, a brother, a name – it was still

hard to take in. And that her twin should be living, that she'd actually seen him, let him go unacknowledged!

In the garden with her letter, Eva looked up into the grey and silvered leaves of the willow which flickered like a shoal of minnows released on the air. A wall had collapsed on Ned Feenan as he walked to church for his wedding. Because of no more than a shoddy bit of brick-laying he, too, was gone with the wind, her father.

Poor Nora. And she'd never guessed.

... Had Ned not died on me like that the pair of us would have found a way to manage somehow for he was charmed the wretch when he learnt I was carrying his child and went rushing out to ask the priest to marry us, and he would have laughed like a fool to know there were the two of you on the way with not a thought of the expense entering his head, which was Ned all over who was joyous and careless like yourself. One time he had the gall to tell me money was only money and I hit him for it, God forgive me, but we had none.

So never imagine you were not wanted Evie or that I did not do what I could which was to stay near, but Aileen would not have the truth told for fear of the neighbours and the Priest not if she and Dermot were to keep you, even to that tale of yourself in a bit of an old shawl on the doorstep which scalded me and laying out half a guinea on a lawful oath that nothing was to be divulged until after their death and my own, she having the mind of a shrivelled-pea and he but a biteen of a man, God between us and all harm. It was a hard bargain and an offence to me but it was that or lose you entirely as I had to lose my boy for she could take only the one and I chose you. If I could have brought myself to let on to be ashamed which I was not the Charity Sisters would have helped me to another situation for I had been dismissed without a character from my last, but why would I bend my neck to a set of old nuns who fancied Ned to be roasting in Hell which was waiting for myself also for no more than the pleasure we had taken in each other. If this seems hard for you to

211

understand Evie remember times were not always as they are now. It was marriage or nothing with a child afford it or not and the Priest with his eye on you from girlhood to make sure you did your duty after and not before the event. If I could have brought you both up myself on what I got for the scrubbing and the laundry I would have done that thing but wouldn't the Priest have had me run out of town for a hussy to be an example to others.

You will realise that Sean is my grief after Ned with no more than the name of a lawyer to link us, but the Feenans were decent people if narrow and I believe that for Ned's sake they will have done right by his son though I was never let clap eyes on my own boy after or communicate in any way, that being the agreement which I have honoured and much good may it do them, but when I die please God things will be out in the open at last as I have always prayed for.

Frank Knapp has my will and instructions to get in touch with Sean. There is the money invested which Uncle Gerald Hogan left me twenty-five years back but since it came too late to save my babies I had no heart in it and never touched so much as a penny piece so it goes to your brother and yourself Evie equally divided and it is my hope that the pair of you will come to mean much to each other. Remember that I never did grow out of a loving memory of your father nor he I think of me for I find Ned under my feet at every turn and you must tell Sean this. Try to help the boy and make him understand how things were and all the hardships, but say above all the only thing I ever was ashamed of was marrying Pringle.

With deep affection from your devoted Mother,
Nora Hogan

P.S. Evie you have much of my Ned in you both his excess of nature and his own wry luck which is why I fuss and worry so. I write this in the hope that death will not be long waiting on me so that you can know the

*truth which I would have told you before my daughter
if I honourably could.*

Eva looked again at the date. Nora had been in the
Keepsake Home less than a month when she had written this.

She moved restlessly across the lawn, sat on the seat
under the plum tree, got up again. His own wry luck! If
only she'd read Nora's letter straight away; if only
she'd known, how warmly she'd have welcomed him,
that brother of hers, when he stood before her, watchful
and expectant. And that he should have gone away
believing himself rejected, yet again rejected. . . .

Oh, but she must put it right!

Eva ran back to the house and leafed through the
directory for Frank Knapp's private number; then, sitting on the edge of her bed, she dialled, the fringes of
her fingers charged with joy as though her brother's
hand was already within reach. But Frank Knapp was
not available. A recorded message directed her to ring
his office on Monday morning.

A little deflated, but only a little, for time would
pass and bring Monday with it; but a little deflated all
the same, because, like a child, she wanted her treat
now, Eva sighed and looked again at the photograph.
And how had Nora felt to see Ned perpetuated in her,
to be forced to observe in silence that gene-carried
stance, the defiant grin? And did Sean hold himself
thus, like their father, like herself? She hadn't
noticed, had seen no more than a hauntingly-familiar
face whose origin evaded her. Only connect. . . .
Forster, yes, but which book? Could it be *A Passage
to India*? She must read Forster again. She must read
again.

But she had a brother, a twin! The knowledge burst
on her afresh like golden rain. Life wasn't all behind
her, life was tomorrow and now; which was the marvellous thing with life, it lay burning about one waiting
only for its fire to be seized. His own wry luck? Yes,
but what great fortune, too, to have blazed with such

213

intensity that Nora had seen him still between the empty doorposts, in the vacant chair.

Too restless to sit, she was up again at once. She'd get down to clipping the grass. Besides, if Mrs Breem wasn't coming any more, then she ought to clean – but, oh, no, not while the sun was shining, for what a waste that would be! Eva picked up the litter bin as she left, remembering with a sudden bruise at the heart what lay inside. But that was yesterday, she told herself as stoutly as she could, and this is now and it's sunny in the garden.

So out she went to it, that wilderness of plenty which she so much loved.

Her eyes half-closed with sunshine, Eva looked about her. The plum tree fountained on to an extravagance of grass which lapped away like green water to break against the exuberant flowers. This was where the farmhouse piggery had once stood, where now great massed choirs crowded to the wall, stretching their necks in praise of dirt and light – campanula, phlox, geum, nigella, achillea, cheiranthus and thrusting, precocious roses shining like angels, like archangels, like all the company of heaven, with big-bloused poppies intruding, a party of worldly ladies, among the high and Anglican lupin spires. And away down there – what could it be, that gleaming mass, John Pipering it beyond the herb bed? Buttercups! Buttercups by the Midas-million! Weeds, but beautiful beyond belief. So how right, sometimes, to let well alone.

Her eyes lifted, then, to the blind windows next door. And ill? Should one sometimes let ill alone, too? How was one to know?

Sobered, Eva turned towards the house; then 'Oh!' she exclaimed, for a child was watching her from the path.

The little girl stood her ground. She could be eight or nine, perhaps – plump, freckled, self-assured; not a child she recognised, not a neighbour's child.

'Hello!' Eva said.

The child stared up at her.

'Is it you that's my auntie?'

214

Astonished, Eva searched the well-scrubbed face. Far brighter than this gaudy melon flower was all that came to her distracted mind.

'Because, if it is, will you be letting my da in, please? He's fit to be tied.'

'Your da?' Eva said faintly.

'He's at the door.' She took Eva's hand. 'That's a grand garden ye have. Why is there writing on your house, Auntie? My da's just after getting in a fight along of it.'

'In a fight? Your father?' It was as unreal as a nightmare, and as immediate. 'So who are you, then?' she asked, not daring to believe.

'I'm Brigid Feenan. I've never been to a foreign place before, and last night didn't I eat my tea in a cafeteria and sleep in a bed on the boat.'

Dazed, Eva looked down at the hand which lay in hers. Then the side gate opened.

'Biddy! Come away out of that; there's nobody home.'

'My auntie's in the garden, Da!'

Eva dropped the child's hand and, overwhelmed with unreality, went forward to meet him, that stranger, the man she'd thought of as Nora's relative, Sean, her twin.

He was standing awkwardly by the gate. One cheek was nicked and his right eye already closing. He wore the same dark suit.

'Oh, you're hurt . . .!'

'Which is nothing to what I did to that young thug.' Defensive, he tried to tidy his hair. 'I can't be doing with violence.'

She meant it as a joke but she was overcome by shyness: 'I wouldn't have guessed' – her voice sounded brittle – 'not from the look of you.'

He jerked as though she'd slapped his face.

'Aren't you very English,' he said after a moment. 'But, then, why wouldn't you be?'

There was both constraint and bitterness there. He held back and, recalling the funeral, she faltered, too.

215

Feeling her hesitate, he flushed. But how begin to explain? Besides, sixty years of separation had washed between herself and her brother. How had she imagined that such a barrier could be breached with an easy kiss?

'Well, there it is. I hit him foolish; and the neighbours were gawping, of course,' he said, depressed. 'Besides which there was regrettable language. . . .' He scowled and fiddled with his tie, and she watched him, numb. 'Ah, for God's sake, woman!' he exploded. 'Aren't I trying to tell you I'm sorry for making more scandal on top of what ye already had, for I can see ye've troubles enough!'

'Scandal?' Eva echoed. Then suddenly she relaxed. It was true; he was here – the wonder of it! Explanations could wait. '*Scandal?*' Impulsively, she seized his arm. 'But scandal's meat and drink to me!'

'Is it now?' He eyed her uncertainly; then, slowly, he began to grin back at the mirror image of his own grin. 'Well, and aren't those the very words I'm come from Dublin to hear!'

27

Dear Idris,

This will be a surprise to you, but I would very much like to meet you if you would be willing to see me. I won't apologise. . . .

She struck out I *won't apologise*, for that wasn't the point. The point was that Idris Lloyd was still alive. She'd found him smiling out at her from the *Irish Times* which Sean had left in the hall. Plumper, older, certainly grander – the paper had reverent things to say about a recent success at Harvard; so would he, now so grand, have forgotten the existence of Eva Wootton? She grinned sadly. No, he would not. He probably stuck a pin in her wax image every day.

She knew where she was going now. The plan had been in her mind since morning, enticing in its obviousness and simplicity. But the letter to Idris was harder to write than she'd have believed possible, and she kept losing touch with herself among its defensive circumlocutions.

'Oh, to hell with it!' she told Pussy; and, screwing up yet another sheet of paper, she started again and wrote the letter at a gulp.

Dear Idris,

All right, the cheek of the woman; but I need your advice and no one else will do. I am moving to Dublin, possibly in mid - June, and intend to resume my inter-rupted studies in the new academic year. Should I try for Trinity or UCD? And whom should I read under, given any choice?

You will no doubt be appalled to hear – she grinned as she wrote – *that I am still vigorous. My memory is no worse than it was except for things like phone numbers and whether the kettle's on and Win a Dream Home; and I know myself to be the richer for my folly. I have plenty of money. My mother*, she wrote with pride, *left me far more than I expect ever to need. What I want now is to have you raging at me again, eyeball to eyeball, which I valued almost above everything who owe you more than you will ever know or I repay.*

As I said at the beginning, the cheek of the woman; but Sonnet 87, line 6 – William, who else? – is in my mind as I write.

I would like to meet you and am free to travel to whatever place you might name at whatever time you pick. Please see me.

Eva

You knew me as Wootton but I am now using Hogan, my true name, which is news to me, too. When you have recovered from your reasonable wrath you may write to me as that. (REASONABLE wrath? Wrath alone will, of course, do. Don't let's start by quarrelling. I long to see you. E.)

And Idris would meet her; he wouldn't be able to resist; though nothing was going to be easy – certainly the work she proposed to undertake couldn't be anything but formidable. Still, as she'd pointed out to Idris last time, formidable and impossible were different things; and, no doubt, obstinacy would again see her through.

Besides, they weren't lost, those years. Nothing in life was ever lost; even dirt from pigs had its rightful place in a garden. It was, rather, as though she'd passed a decade, dazed among archives, researching her chosen study, which, when written, would make sense of all those scrawled notes and jotted fragments.

But that she should now have the means to take up that broken end! Eva hadn't at first noticed the fact of money, though Nora had stated it clearly enough. It was Sean, grave, still shaken by the information, who told her just how much; for Frank Knapp had murmured a figure, hoping to cheer him on the day of the funeral when – or so it had seemed to the two men – his twin would have none of him.

They'd been able to talk about it then; and Sean had understood, had admitted he'd have been at a loss himself were he not already in the know. And what with the shock and the emotion and travelling all night and the bloody heat – well, Evie could see how it was. By the time he'd gathered his wits it was too late. He'd had to wait for the Saturday boat before he could come roaring back to tell that sister of his to have sense. Because there might be money but it wasn't yet, and he'd a wife and a family to keep. . . .

'Are there other children? How many, Sean?'

And looking like their father in that yellowed snap he'd tossed his head at her and said defiantly: 'Siven!'

So, he went on, when was Evie coming over to meet that family of hers?

When was she coming? As soon as she could, of course; but she must get rid of the house first.

But at least she'd spend Christmas with them?

Christmas? Let anyone try to stop her!

And then to find Idris's face looking out from the *Irish Times.* . . .

The decision had come into her head, fully-formed, along with Forster's only connect; and even before she'd begun to consider how she was going to pay for her studies she'd accepted that that was what she should do. The intermission was over. It was time for the last act to begin.

They hadn't had long together, her brother and she, and those hours had gone on photographs, the trivia of catching up, new names; but in that brief space it seemed as though the need of a lifetime had been met.

219

She was still a woman alone when she longed to be part of a couple. She had lost her lover and dared not yet contemplate the full devastation of that loss. But she knew who she was now. She was Eva Hogan; and as Eva Hogan she could face tomorrow with some equanimity.

THE END

Jumping The Queue
Mary Wesley

'A virtuoso performance of guileful plotting, deft
characterization and malicious wit'
THE TIMES

Matilda Poliport, recently widowed, has decided to End It
All. But her meticulously planned bid for graceful oblivion
is foiled, and when later she foils the suicide attempt of
another lost soul – Hugh Warner, on the run from the
police – life begins again for both.

But life also begins to throw up nasty secrets and
awkward questions: just what was Matilda's husband
Tom doing in Paris? How is the soon-to-be-knighted John
(or Piers as he likes to be called) involved? Was Louise
more than just a lovely daughter? And why did Hugh
choose Matilda as his saviour?

Jumping the Queue is a brilliantly written first novel
brimming over with confidence and black humour,
reminiscent of Muriel Spark at her magnificent best.

'Great verve and inventiveness . . . (Matilda is) a
convincing original'
TIMES LITERARY SUPPLEMENT

0 552 99082 5

BLACK SWAN

Harnessing Peacocks
Mary Wesley

'Delightful, intelligent entertainment'
THOMAS HINDE, SUNDAY TELEGRAPH

Hebe listens in the darkness of the hall to a family conference. The stern hypocrisy of her grandfather is winning the day. He has summoned her three horsey sisters' successful husbands and they are discussing Hebe's unexpected pregnancy. The decision, unanimous, is that it be terminated. Hebe, dissenting, flees into the night.

Twelve summers later she is living happily alone with her son in a seaside town in Cornwall. He is receiving an expensive education. Hebe has organised her life oddly but well. She has two chief talents in life – cooking and making love – and these she has exercised with dignity, in privacy and for profit.

It is when the separate strands of the web of Hebe's life become entangled that the even tenor of her days is threatened, and her life is changed.

HARNESSING PEACOCKS, Mary Wesley's third novel, is suffused with freshness, warmth and wit. The author's delightful literary skills are here fully engaged in a story of independence, honesty and sensual charm.

'Mary Wesley goes from strength to strength . . . She has a great zest for life . . . The book is tremendously lively, very funny, touching, spirited'
SUSAN HILL, GOOD HOUSEKEEPING

0 552 99210 0

BLACK SWAN

Brother of the More Famous Jack
Barbara Trapido

'A sort of Bohemian *Brideshead Revisited*'
TIMES LITERARY SUPPLEMENT

Here are the Goldmans: Jacob, born in London's Jewish ghetto, and now an eminent professor of philosophy, and wife, Jane, an acid-tongued earth-mother who rocked her aristocratic family by going off to live with Jacob in bohemian squalor. We enter their ebullient, untidy world through Katherine, a student of Jacob's who falls in love with the oldest Goldman child. When the affair ends badly, Katherine flees to Rome, determined to put them *all* behind her. But she returns, ten years later, seasoned and more knowing, to discover that their lives are inextricably bound, that old wounds do heal, and that life goes forward in all its deep and satisfying bounty.

A wry, elegant and involving novel that introduces a major new talent to the world of literature.

'I hope it is stocked by railway-station bookstalls. I hope railway-station bookstalls have to build extensions to house the necessary copies'
FINANCIAL TIMES

'The style is hectic and passionate, the jokes thick and fast, the emotions full and right, the humanity total and engulfing . . . a first fruit to savour and exalt'
THE TIMES

'Its high spirits are irresistible. Like Moll Flanders, the heroine is unstoppable'
SUNDAY TELEGRAPH

0 552 99056 6

BLACK SWAN

Noah's Ark
Barbara Trapido

NOAH'S ARK is a wry and sparkling account of a
marriage: an apparently incompatible union between Noah
Glazer, a solid man of science, and Alison Bobrow, a
palely captivating eccentric, who Noah suspects of
'keeping a Tarot Pack in the bureau drawer'. For both the
marriage – after a memorably sexy and precipitous
courtship implies a serious departure from type. Noah
walks undaunted into the overpopulated labyrinth of
Alison's life, coolly issuing forth the unspeakable maxim
that 'Charity begins at Home'. The result is serenity and
order, until Alison is drawn to explore certain avenues in
her past. The consequences are both hectic and
illuminating. . . .

NOAH'S ARK, with its lively wit, its piquant insight and
its varied and outrageous characters, more than fulfils the
promise of the prize-winning BROTHER OF THE MORE
FAMOUS JACK (also available in Black Swan)

'An achingly funny novel . . . wickedly observed'
LIBBY PURVES, LIVING

'Witty and highly polished . . . never a dull moment'
ALANNAH HOPKIN, THE STANDARD

'Zesty, intelligent and highly readable'
DEBORAH MOGGACH, COSMOPOLITAN

'Reading it is rather like being bombarded by sequins'
ANTHONY THWAITE, THE OBSERVER

0 552 99130 9

BLACK SWAN